About the Author

Anthony Ferner is a former professor of international business and is published widely in non-fiction in his field. He has one other published novella, called *Winegarden*.

T0148760

First published by Fairlight Books 2018

Fairlight Books
Summertown Pavilion,
18 - 24 Middle Way,
Oxford, OX2 7LG

Copyright © Anthony Ferner 2018

The right of Anthony Ferner to be identified as the author of this work has been asserted by Anthony Ferner in accordance with the Copyright, Designs and Patents Act 1988.

All rights reserved. This book is copyright material and must not be copied, stored, distributed, transmitted, reproduced or otherwise made available in any form, or by any means (electronic, digital, optical, mechanical, photocopying, recording or otherwise) without the prior written permission of the publisher.

A CIP catalogue record for this book is available from the British Library

1 2 3 4 5 6 7 8 9 10

ISBN 978-1-912054-54-1

www.fairlightbooks.com

Printed and bound in Great Britain by Clays Ltd, Elcograf S.p.A.

Designed by Sara Wood

Illustrated by Sam Kalda
www.folioart.co.uk

Inside the Bone Box

ANTHONY FERNER

Fairlight Books

Captain America

Nicholas Anderton shuffled his bulk the few hundred yards along the promenade from the hotel to the conference centre. Most days he would have taken a taxi, but this morning he felt a need to make amends, however perfunctory, for the dinner he'd eaten the night before. He'd gone for seafood, the healthy option: spider crab, mussels in a peppery sauce, followed by the equally healthy grilled wild turbot (normally for two). But then, the cheeses, the puddings, the bottle or two of slightly *pétillant* Txakoli, the digestifs...

He walked slowly; any kind of exercise seemed a form of expiation. The town intimidated him. It was the kind of Basque resort where even a gathering of neurosurgeons could be seen as lowering the tone. Every few minutes, he paused to look out to sea and catch his breath. He leant heavily on the cast iron railings, wondering if they might give way. Far off in the bay, kite surfers, clad in their costumes of fluorescent limes and yellows, skimmed the waters in the breeze. Anderton's son Ben had told him that kite surfing was like skiing, with a touch of paragliding to it, but more fun than either: Ben was annoyingly sporty, so like his mother in her youth, so unlike his father. No, Anderton was not one for sport; yet he did wonder what it might be like if he too could soar and dip in the wind.

Ben was already a promising young scientist, a future high-flyer, creating new compounds to untangle the curling protein clumps of dementing brains. His sister, Sophie, was more prosaic and earthbound, aggressive-defensive and a little frightened of things, but wishing like Ben to change the world, even if she was still unsure how. A memory: Sophie and Ben aged five and four, in their superhero outfits; she as Batman, 'because he's a real person, Daddy,' and he as Spiderman, because webs were cool...

Anderton smiled sadly. He too had once set out to change the world. But now, not yet fifty, he would catch glimpses of himself in shop windows, too fat and ponderous to change anything, even himself, and would wonder, astonished, how it had come to this. What could he now aspire to, or hope for, other than to become heavier, slower, less good at what he did? The conference was a short respite from the pressures of work, the meeting with the clinical director when he returned to London, decisions to be made. Respite too from the strains at home, his wife Alyson growing thinner and more irritable as he expanded. He'd look in the gift shops, find something to take back for her. Jewellery perhaps, or a print of the bay with its wooded island. And some saffron, tablets of nougat. Not alcohol. How long to go till the lunch break, he wondered.

He watched the kite surfers cavort, saw how they used the slope of the waves to take off, and twist and turn and somersault through the air; their kites darted across the sky like a flock of birds. He felt the acid reflux below his heart, and a stab of resentment towards these beings who could so lightly defy gravity.

He continued, sweating with the exertion, and with the heat of the sun as it rose above the *belle époque* buildings behind him. Mouth agape like a giant tortoise, he laboured around the sweep of the bay, past the haughty cream façades of the Hotel de Viena and the Hotel Inglaterra, past the wrought ironwork, tiles and arched windows of the Reina Victoria theatre, and reached at last the foot of the wooded hill at the far western end of the beach.

On the seaward side, the hill fell away steeply, and the almost sheer face was terraced and lined with grand mansions. At the summit was the conference venue, an old building tastefully modernised, accessible from the seafront by lift. It had wide plate-glass windows that looked out on the bay. They bore the painted silhouettes of hawks in order, Anderton guessed, to deter gulls and pigeons from dashing themselves against the panes. He took the lift to the top of the cliff and climbed the wide entrance steps of the conference centre, anxious now to find somewhere cool to sit and to have refreshments laid out for him. As he entered the building, a gust of breeze stirred the bushes on the forecourt.

*

The programme for the morning dealt with neuro-surgical errors and disasters. Speakers expounded on risk-minimising checklists, protocols and procedures. In his seat at the end of a row, beside the only one of the expansive windows not obscured by dark blinds, Anderton drummed his fingers on the notepad. Had he not been asked to contribute to a panel discussion after the coffee break, he might well have stayed in the hotel, enjoyed a leisurely amble through the hot and cold buffet. What were they whingeing on for? Surgery was risky, damn it. Surgical arrogance was necessary for progress, not some defect of character to be confined by rules. Sauerbruch, for example. If he hadn't taken risks, thoracic surgery would still be in the dark ages. True, he supported the National Socialists and, in his later years, operated on patients upon his kitchen table with boning knives. But so what? Progress required victims, sacrificial offerings. Think of Bill Scoville, the old rogue. He sucked out poor Henry Molaison's hippocampus. Cured his seizures, destroyed his memory. No pain, no gain. Scoville took flak for that, but we know so much more about memory these days...

Anderton gazed out of the window. He had a fine view of the full curve of the bay. The waves had stiffened, with belligerent white crests, and the trees on the promenade were swaying. The conference speaker droned on. You learn from your mistakes, Anderton thought. Except when you don't, when the never events happen. Such as the time his junior inserted a nasogastric tube into a trauma patient and, instead of going down the man's oesophagus to suck out the contents of his stomach, it passed inadvertently through a thin, fractured bone at the top of the nasal cavity and into the brain; it coiled itself tightly there and aspirated a good portion of the cerebral tissue, like a soft white curd. A rare mistake, but with terrible consequences, at least for the patient. He sighed. He'd made his own mistakes, big ones: less gross, perhaps, but even more inexcusable. No point dwelling on them, though.

A soughing of wind was just audible through the window panes. It rose and fell away and rose again. Fat raindrops were beginning to spatter the glass. Anderton looked out and saw that the trees on the front were bending hard towards the landward side. And in the length of time it had taken for his mind to wander from white curd to the prospect of lunch, the sky had grown dark, the rain coming in squally bursts with clouds pushing in from the Bay of Biscay. Sunbathers were scampering up the sand in search of shelter.

The lecturer, a local man, looked up at the sound of the rain dashing against the windows. He gazed out at the black massing clouds. '*La galerna,*' he said. 'The sea wind. Don't worry, in a few minutes it will be sunny again. Meanwhile, you are better in here than out there.' He returned to his data: a 7 per cent reduction in post-operative complications in neurosurgery in 2014 as a result of following the WHO checklist and guidelines, with a p-value of...

Anderton watched distant kite surfers lift from the agitated sea and blow about like sycamore seeds, gyrating then soaring at the mercy of the breeze until they were lost from sight. He enjoyed a moment of schadenfreude.

There was a shuddering bang in the auditorium. The delegates cried out and looked at each other in alarm; some rose from their seats. Terrorism was always at the back of people's minds, even here. Anderton saw a kite-surfer being whipped savagely away from the building by the wind. The fellow must have been blown into the façade of the conference centre, struck the plate glass at a shallow angle, and bounced off again, surging seaward.

Before the speaker could resume, another powerful gust brought the surfer back towards the building and he crashed through the glass close to where Anderton sat. Shards sprayed over the audience. The surfer thudded to the floor and lay still.

There was a moment of stasis, as if the event was too outlandish to make sense of, and then a buzz of

10

noise as delegates in the front row hurried to attend the splayed, face-down body. Two or three figures huddled round the victim, exchanging urgent suggestions in accented English. They seemed uncertain as they turned him over, more used to intricate work in theatre than to the messy, lowly demands of first aid.

Anderton rose from his seat and joined the group around the injured man. He kneeled, wincing at the sharp twinges in his joints. At first, he did not notice the blood on the man's wrists, where arteries had been severed by sharp edges of glass, as the man was wearing red gauntlets.

Indeed, what shocked and unsettled Anderton was that the surfer was dressed in a superhero outfit. Gradually the red and white vertical stripes on the abdomen of his costume turned a more uniform red. The spreading dampness dyed almost purple the blue of the material stretched tight across his chest. Red welled too at his throat and at his temple, staining the blue headpiece with its large white 'A', which they now gingerly removed.

Anderton bent forwards and touched two fingers to the side of the victim's neck, sensed the fading pulse. He had an unexpected spurt of fellow feeling for this poor fish out of water. Afterwards, what stayed with him was the look on the young man's face: an expression of astonishment that such a fate could be visited upon Captain America, that it had come to this.

Alyson

Alyson dozes in the armchair, a glass of wine on the low table in front of her. She wakes, taking deep slow breaths. Imagines she's on a desert island. Sees herself lying on a beach of white sand beneath tall palms whose canopies sway in the breeze. Luscious ripples of air cool and stroke her burning skin. The waves lap onto the strand with a whooshing, lulling sound, and a little out to sea, beyond the breakers, a fishing boat rises and falls with the gentle swell. She is on the verge of closing her eyes. She's not sure, but perhaps she does close them. She moves her hand, and beneath it there is something unpleasantly gelatinous and moist-cold. She looks down and sees an enormous jellyfish, its transparent body laced with ominous threads of purple. Its trailing tendrils, which she knows to be poisonous, are unbearably close to her skin. She watches herself scramble to her feet in alarm. On the sand as far as the eye can see lies a carpet of thousands, millions, of these creatures, and she is trapped.

She shakes her head. She feels sick and dehydrated, and rises from the armchair, goes to the kitchen, pours herself a large glass of water. She thinks of Nick, with his breathless bulk. He used to be firm; now he's pale and repellent, and he wobbles, he vibrates.

She's tracked Anderton's weight since they met, can spout his statistics: a solid 83 kilos as a student (in old money, 13 stone), never sylphlike, but he wore it well, light on his feet. A chunky 95 kilos aged forty, a bit of flab but bearable. Then came the challenges of his mid-career, of their faltering mid-lives together, and now, at almost fifty, he's a quivering 128 kilos, with a body mass index of 39-point-something. And it's not just him she monitors: she obsessively weighs herself too, same time every day, before breakfast, after a shit. Not that she shits regularly these days. Anyway, she's not a gram heavier than when she was thirty, since before she had the kids, even.

She has this recurring vision that she can't get out of her head, of stepping on him in her bare feet and feeling his slimy, slug-jellyfish contents on her own skin. She longs for the hard flesh she used to enjoy, for what seemed brief moments, aeons ago. In her memory she was engulfed, in those days, by lust. And later, again, and more briefly still... When she found out about him and that scrub nurse, and the other women, she could have cut his bits off. With the kitchen scissors. Or her teeth. She did

13

seriously consider the deed, for an hour or so, before sobering up.

But she's gone through all the anger, the castration fantasies. There'd be little point these days: his prick is like a useless wormy sluglet attached to the enormous mother-slug. What he doesn't use he wouldn't miss. Standing, he couldn't even glimpse the thing over the curvature of his belly.

And yet, and yet. A part of her knows there is a binding together. She still wants him, still feels a fascination when his blue eyes are upon her. His gaze is so frank and direct, even when he's got something to hide. She's always imagined it must be scary for his juniors to be caught in one of his glares. There's something detached about it, something of the bird of prey's cold-eyed assessment. It is, yes, very attractive. In any case, she's tried to leave, more than once, but she hasn't been able to. She hates him for that, for his addictiveness.

This week he's at some neurosurgical congress abroad. She feels less on edge when he's away. Possibly because she has less need to be surreptitious in her drinking. No need to hide the evidence. Though the hiding is more for form's sake, since she knows he knows. Talking of which, maybe he'll bring her back a bottle of Basque liqueur from San Sebastián.

Over a glass of Penedès

Anderton got home from work late, tired. The last operation had gone on much longer than he'd have liked. A tricky subarachnoid haemorrhage. He poured a glass of good Penedès, took a sip and then another, and walked over to kiss his seated wife. She pulled away and crossed her legs, and drank from her glass of white wine.

'Oof. What a day,' he said. 'Horrible operation. Like trying to find your way in a bloody mangrove swamp. Bloody mess in there.'

Alyson didn't respond. He sank into the sofa, stomach spreading. He was developing a definite dewlap, like those African cattle. He set his glass on the armrest, held up his hands and examined them with a puzzled expression, as if they'd let him down. On a good day at work, the tips of his fingers seemed to tingle with focused energy. They sensed the space, rose, turned through angles, intuited the tissue, felt the consistency of flesh, used just the right degree of delicacy or brutality. The tiny instruments, seen through the neurosurgical microscope, were extensions of him, of his skilful fingers. He could stand at the operating table and twiddle the probe within the corpus callosum with surprising finesse, like a chimpanzee tickling for grubs in the bark of a tree with a twig. In the early days, when he and Alyson had begun to sleep together, she'd say, 'You've a good touch, for a big man.' She corrected herself: 'A good touch, for a *man*.'

His wife was looking at him now, one arm tightly crossed over her chest, the other gripping her glass within sipping distance.

'Cheers,' he said, thrusting his glass in her direction.

She made no move. She said, trying to enunciate with care, 'You're fat, you've grown fat, you weren't fat when I married you.' The word 'fat' seemed too full for her mouth.

'So you have a problem with fat.'

'I have a problem with fat.'

'Hold the front page, Alyson has a...'

'Not part of the contract, fat.'

'Darling, I have a problem with *thin*. I hate the way you take scrawniness for a virtue. Anyway, I don't try to be fat, it just happens.'

'I think you do try to be fat, the way you cram food into your face. All bloody day long.'

'That's arguable. Whereas you do definitely try to be thin.' And drunk, he thought.

'You're so fat you can't even fuck me any more.'

It was true: his *Parts Noble* (as he thought of

16

them, in almost heraldic terms) had been stood down from active service for a while now. He noted her changing line of attack. For years, before he became so grossly overweight, it would be, 'If you're screwing that curvy-arsed registrar of yours, Nick...' She meant 'curvy-arsed' as the ultimate insult. 'Or is it a radiographer this time? Or a nurse, God help us.' When drunk, she'd add, slurring, 'You're a bastard, Anderton.'

'Why are we together?' she said. 'Remind me.' The subtext was that she could have any number of younger, trimmer men.

'I don't know. We're like an incompatible role-reversed Mr and Mrs Sprat.'

She exhaled contemptuously. It was often like this now the kids had grown up, left home; though poor Sophie was still needy, and they both missed her more than they'd expected.

'I've spoken to Rabinovich,' he said.

'Who?'

'Phil Rabinovich, my colleague, the consultant surgeon in gastroenterology.'

She seemed to sober up. 'The boys' club? And?'

'Spoken to him about a stomach clamp. A gastric band.'

'What about it?'

'About having one. Me having one.'

'A gastric band? You? Are you mad! That could kill you.'

'Or make me thinner. Either way you'd be happy.'

She drank some wine. 'But you're not doing it for me.'

'Ha! What makes you say that?'

'Because it's not like you. I know you.' She appraised him with her small bright eyes; like a malign vole, he thought.

'Nothing's decided. I'm considering.'

'It's because you're frightened they'll stop you operating unless you lose weight. Isn't that it?'

'You're the pits,' he said, hauling himself up and walking effortfully from the room.

'Your thighs rub together,' she called after him. 'You could make fire.'

He held up a hand, middle finger pointing to the ceiling; because she was right, they did rub together. Had they always done that? He heard her cackle, wanted to say, *You're a bastard, Alyson.*

Alyson

Alyson stands in the middle of the room, her fingers tightening on the bowl of her glass. She hates the way Nick brings out the worst in her. She wants to cry, and wishes she had someone to talk to, to confide in, not merely to exchange poisoned barbs with. He winds her up, but that's better than his not winding her up, not attending to her at all, the long silent spells. She misses Sophie. They could have curled up on the settee together, close enough to touch, chatting. But Sophie's gone to the Midlands to work, and in any case, since leaving behind the frayed comfort blanket of home, she's become even more spiky and fragile, less use. What's the point of a daughter if you can't do mother–daughter stuff together? Sophie will talk to him more than she'll talk to her mother.

So, no one to talk to.

In the meantime, Alyson thinks, she'll talk to the glass.

Out of shame and bloody pride, she's waited until he's out of sight before taking down the bottle of vodka from the bookshelf and topping up her white wine to the brim. She contemplates the delicious paleness of the liquid, and waits. It's like when you're desperate for a pee: you've scoured the city for a loo, at last you've found one, with no queue, tolerably clean, and you've gone into a cubicle and locked the door. And for a luxurious moment you wait astride the bowl, anticipating the imminent relief. So now, finally, she does drink, deeply, and her taut body relaxes. She hears him in the other room open the fridge door.

She thinks, 'He could die, fuck it, he could die.'

*

She strains against the dead weight of her eyelids to awaken. She is sitting at an uncomfortable angle on the leather armchair in the living room with a novel open face down beside her and on the coffee table there is an empty wine glass. Next to it is an empty bottle of white wine in a pitcher of melted ice. She feels panic as she scans the shelves. But there, towards the top, is the bottle of vodka, still nearly half full, and she can relax. She will not have to drive anywhere in this state to find a Spar still open. She could go to prison, even, if they stopped her over the limit again. Not long ago, she knocked a man off his bike. He got up, thank God, and swore at her. She's more careful now, she tries to stock up.

There's no sign of Nick. She sinks back against the armchair and becomes aware of a coolness under her. She has wet herself. The first time, a few months back, she put it down to fatigue, a urinary tract infection, the stress at work. She convinced herself it was a one-off and wouldn't happen again. Now it has. She feels disgust, a sense of being trapped by abhorrent organic substances. She gets up. She knows there are only two ways out, and that one of those is no way out at all; she wouldn't have the guts. So, only the one way out. It's been coming, the pieces have been stacking up. And now: Nick going for the operation.

She rises, circumnavigates the coffee table, unsteady on her feet, and goes upstairs to wash and change. She comes back down and wipes the leather clean and mops the floor. On her hands and knees, she rubs polish into the parquet, and rises and sniffs the air: no hint of urine. To make sure, she opens the big bay window and a gust of cool air rushes in. At least she has not lost control of her bowels. Not yet, at any rate.

But she can't go on like this. Can she?

The warm pulse of her

A year or two before the San Sebastián conference, a young woman had come into Anderton's consulting room. She reminded him of Sophie; not so much in looks, more in her way of being in the world, her fragility, her vulnerability with edge. Her questions had a knowing sharpness, as if she expected him to let her down.

Her tumour was benign, but as it grew it would threaten vital structures. There were risks: it was in a tricky position and reaching it was not straightforward. 'I know there are always risks,' she said. They all said that, as if by acknowledging the dangers they could avert them.

'Particular risks,' said Anderton. 'Higher than usual risks of worse than normal outcomes.'

She repeated the word 'outcomes' as if it were an affront, angry at him for being the bearer of bad news. He saw her staring at his bulk and became uncomfortably conscious of his belly, the stretched tightness of the trouser fabric over his thighs, the girth of his forearms.

'It's coming for me anyway,' she said. 'It's one risk against another, isn't it?'

He waited. As a less-experienced doctor he would have leaped in, responded to the question. But he knew that she was coming to a decision.

'I want it,' she said at last.

He nodded.

'Don't mess it up.' Perhaps she'd meant her tone to be light, jokey, but it sounded forced.

'We'll do the best we can,' he said.

But then it was as if the uncertainties struck her afresh. 'And what happens if I do nothing?'

'It depends. How fast the tumour grows, how close it gets to...'

As she talked through her anxieties, he fixed his eyes on a reddening spot on her chin that marred her features, and his attention started to wander. Wandered above all to Sophie, and her current dull dog of a boyfriend: some sub-species of gym-toned, aspirational marketing manager whose mind and ambitions ran on tramlines. Charles, he called himself. Anderton had seen the photo on social media. The fellow's arm was around Sophie, proprietorially, staking his claim, his mouth set in an idiot grin. She was wearing a party frock and high heels, was carefully made up, carefully sub-missive. What had happened, Anderton wondered, to his prickly, mouthy, insurgent daughter? He told himself it wasn't that he was afraid to let her go, merely reluctant to abandon her to this bland nonentity who would no doubt burr away what was interesting about her.

*

Now the tumour patient lay on the operating table. Anderton saw before him only a small patch of exposed scalp, dyed yellow with antiseptic amid the surgical drapes: not a person but a technically arduous task, to be accomplished with professional detachment. The skull was drilled, the dura opened and folded back, and the brain exposed, pulsing softly under the lights, with its tracery of fine blood vessels. This moment still induced in him a sense of the revelation of mysteries.

He sat at the operating microscope, which was large and weighty yet feathery in its responsive, counter-balanced refinement. Like me, he mused, conscious of the gulf between his cumbersome body and his sensitive fingers. This was the time for thought-free concentration, an attention to the immediacy of senses. He did not have to think, because his fingers thought for him, schooled in countless repetitions of each subtle movement until it had become second nature. When Sophie was young, he used to take her on Saturdays to the ice rink for her lesson, and watched the figure skaters endlessly repeat the same move – the three-turn, the twizzle, the rocker, the counter – until the instinctive point of balance was reached, the precise combination of weightings and unweightings, edges and angles, twists of the spine, adjustments of head, hips and arms, that made the move possible.

And so it was now, in miniature, with the life-altering ballet of his fingers.

Guided by the three-dimensional computer images, he navigated the pathways between the lobes. He crawled along fissures, traversed chasms, slipped through ventricles and edged around the obstructions of nerves and veins looming like glistening bluish mangrove roots, until he reached the site of the tumour. This was a benign teratoma the size of a bantam's egg. Within its thick sac it contained a mass of sebaceous material, whitish and foul-smelling, with the consistency in places of clotted cream and elsewhere granular, like brandy butter. He scooped it out with a micro-spoon, and tugged away with minute forceps at the strands of coarse black hair embedded in it.

Because the patient reminded him of Sophie, he took great care, perhaps too much; and at the same time he was more nervous than he should have been. Was that a small tremor of fear agitating the probe within the deflated sac of the tumour? However skilful the surgeon, flesh is resistant, messy. Anatomical features meld into each other, are obscured by seeping blood. Tissue pulls back elastically into your line of sight. Progress can only be halting, through small, patient, repetitive movements until the brain's substances align for long enough to undertake the next move. As he cut the posterior surface of the sac free from the surrounding tissue, his anxiety increased. A mistake could cause a gush of blood that, magnified on the screen, would seem like the torrential bursting of a dam. Too often in his career, Anderton had made mistakes, sometimes unavoidable. Once or twice, his professional competitiveness and arrogance had been punctured by utter disaster. He was conscious of Leriche's famous aphorism about every surgeon dragging around a graveyard peopled with his failed cases. Except that for a neurosurgeon, the graveyard was inevitably not small, and some of the ghosts that populated it were unforgiving.

Anderton would gather his trainee doctors, coming into neurology for a few weeks on their surgical rotation, and would say, his sharp blue eyes trained on them,

How would you feel about killing a man? Or a woman. Or worse, a child with their life ahead of them? If you don't wish to be a killer, don't become a neurosurgeon. Because you are going to kill. And not just once. If you cannot be a hardened killer, you cannot be a saver of lives. Yet when things go wrong, because the brain is intractable and surprises you, and because you are dealing in tiny margins for error, and because you often reach the limits of your skills and your judgement, people will die. You will feel like hell. It may be there was nothing you could have done, but you'll always think you could have done more. Or perhaps you got tired, severed a vital structure, nicked an artery, or knocked the brainstem. Or you were arrogant, believed in your own infallibility, flew too close to the sun... You now have a dead patient or, worse, a live one, horribly incapacitated. Your disasters will eat away at you like a parasite. Since you'll never forgive yourself, all you can do is forget. Repress. The event will slowly fade, especially after the next cock-up, the next fall from grace. The only thing to do is get back in the saddle. Operate again as soon as possible. Carry on. Don't look back.

The trainee medics would glance at each other, half-amused by Anderton's hyperbole, half-fearful for their own clouded futures.

Now, in the operating theatre, he halted his probing in alarm, crying, 'Bloody hell!', thinking that he had cut through the back wall of the tumour into the stuff beyond – the stuff of thought, emotion, life itself. His registrar, peering through the side arm of the microscope, calmed him and assured him it was merely a bulging appendage of the main tumour. Anderton drew in a long breath, moved in his seat, let go of the instruments, took them in his fingers again. He prised the remaining sac of the tumour away from the surrounding tissue without incident. His body slumped in on itself with relief and he left his registrar to finish and close up.

Anderton felt wrung out, and immensely hungry. In his locker he found the remains of a giant bar of fruit and nut chocolate, and ate it for a quick boost to his blood sugar. He left the hospital and walked to Le Frattaglie, the small Italian restaurant round the corner. Its proprietor Gianluca knew him and was, after a fashion, his friend. Anderton could not bear the way other fat men, and women, would approach him at parties, on station platforms, in burger bar queues. They presumed complicity, took for granted that he was one of them, that he shared their guilt and self-loathing. He did not wish to belong to their whingeing commonwealth of the stigmatised. He thought of himself as unrepentant, unapologetic, defiant in his fatness. But Gianluca was different. In Gianluca, with his enormous paunch and gleeful culinary excess, he saw a fellow spirit. The Italian did not judge; he merely facilitated, and for that Anderton was grateful.

Gianluca greeted him with a handshake. 'Ah, Nick, good to see you again, it's been too long.' Anderton sat at his usual table, discreetly out of the way of the stares of other diners. 'All this week,' said Gianluca, 'our special offering for you is offal.' He rubbed his hands. '*Fucking* delicious. I bring you a selection.' Anderton nodded, smiling at his host's off-register English.

He ate *zuppa forte*, a stew made of parts of pig that were not muscle: lung was in there, according to Gianluca, and tripe, trachea, glands. Then, a collection of small plates was brought out, each with its portion of food that Gianluca pointed to and described: bull's testicles, sliced and fried;

lambs' brains in breadcrumbs; veal sweetbreads in butter and sage; pigs' kidneys in white wine. As Anderton finished each item, his host brought more, and waited by the table until he'd tasted them and nodded his appreciation, or occasionally frowned uncertainly. Gianluca was unflustered. 'You don't like it, Nick? No problem, it's not my favourite either. Let's move on.' Anderton ate slowly, relentlessly; drank red wine, in frequent cautious sips. Sometimes he closed his eyes to savour the texture of the meat or grittiness of the polenta, or to capture an elusive flavour of ferrous sweetness, or livery bitterness, or the subtle aroma of a herb, or a surprising hint of saffron. After the meats, Anderton had a generous chunk of *pecorino stravecchio*. He finished the cheese and said, tongue-in-cheek, 'And dessert, Gianluca? Is that offal-based too?'

The Italian looked serious. 'You want, Nick? You're sure?'

'Yes,' said Anderton, 'I think I can make room.'

Gianluca laughed and patted him on the shoulder. 'Of course you can! Good man!' He soon returned with a large bowl of congealing *sanguinaccio:* milk, sugar, chocolate – pig's blood. It had the consistency of setting custard. 'It's beautiful, isn't it?' said Gianluca.

Yes, thought Anderton, *fucking delicious*. The food and wine infused him with new life, eased his tension, allowed him to revel in an extended present moment of the senses in which the past did not gnaw at him, nor future troubles weigh him down. At last he laid aside the napkin, stained with flashes of ochre, garnet, rust and sepia, and got to his feet, clinging to the table edge for support. He felt a momentary urge to stroke his belly, feel the temporarily satisfying fullness there. He paid, and Gianluca accompanied him to the door. Outside it was dark. The two men shook hands; had they been of smaller girth, perhaps they would have embraced.

*

In the night, Anderton awoke on his back, sweating and fighting for breath, as if apnoea had stopped his throat. His mouth was parched from the salty food, and he'd had an unsettling dream: Sophie in front of him, in distress. *This is really serious*, she says, with that panicked aggression he fears and loves in her. *Really serious.* He looks again, and sees that his daughter's face is erupting in angry red sores, weeping pustules. Her eyes are frightened. They stoke dread in him. Her cheeks and forehead are swollen. He has a sense that this is the end. He lays her down on the bed, and lies beside her, his arm around her to comfort her in her final moments. He has not noticed until now how like him she is, how fat. This consoles him in a way he finds hard to explain, though even in his dream a part of him knows that in waking life she is not fat at all. He feels the warm pulse of her, and says, 'We have each other,' and she smiles back at him. For a moment he is content, almost euphoric.

But awake, Anderton felt a desolation he could not shake off, and a burrowing shame. Sleep did not return, so he rose, relieved that he did not have to explain himself to Alyson, now that they had separate bedrooms: 'Your snoring is intolerable,' she'd said. 'If you're a doctor, do something about it, or get something done.' 'Snoring is not a medical condition.' 'Well, it's making me ill,' she'd retorted. 'Go and sleep in another room. Christ, it's not as if you're any use to me in bed.'

He sat at the bedroom table and turned on his laptop. He sought out Sophie's Facebook page, surprised as always that she had not blocked him, found her photograph with Charles, and stared at it for a long time, as if taking his leave. He scrolled down through her photos, back to her late teenage years. Her poses before she met Charles were always defiant, assertive, vulnerable: his Sophie. Then, remorseful but resentful, he forced himself to cut his links to her account, to unfriend her. The dream had been a reproach, and this small gesture might hold at bay the bad stuff a while longer.

Later, he flicked from website to website filled with women in postures of submission, backs to the camera, bent over, exposed, peering round to pout at him, to incite him to imagined acts of penetration. But he felt no desire, just a frustrated numbness.

Anderton closed the laptop and went out onto the landing. He would take a shower. Baths were a trial these days, both the getting in and the getting out. Even showers were not easy. With his stiff shoulders and hips, he found it difficult to reach round behind him, soap his buttocks, his intimate parts, direct the spray from the shower head. He envisaged the day when he would need to devise some contraption, some aid to daily living: a washcloth attached to the end of a curving loofah brush, perhaps. Or did such things already exist?

He showered as best he could and dried himself – a lengthy task. He took care to move aside folds of flesh, dab the skin, sprinkle talcum powder. Some of this he did lying on the bed, wriggling awkward-ly into position, sometimes flopping helplessly like a beached sea creature. Dressing took the same focus and contortions. He had to remember to thread the belt through his trousers before putting them on, being unable to encompass the circumference of himself. His waist size had expanded in a few years from 39 inches to the high-40s, and he had learned the paradox of the fat man: that the bulging gut does not help to hold up the trousers but sends them slip-ping down the hips, while the shirttail rides up to expose the crack between the buttocks. So he now wore braces, invariably bright red or yellow, to com-plement his navy suits. He manoeuvred into his socks by sitting on the edge of the bed, bringing one foot onto a footstool and easing the sock over the toes with one hand reaching. On bad days, his feet seemed far off from his arms, the gulf unbridgeable.

Dressed at last, he shuffled down the stairs, his right foot leading at every step and his knees rebelling. In the kitchen he moved from fridge to fruit bowl to fitted cupboards, gathering foodstuffs, anticipating the comforts of a very early breakfast.

Alyson

Alyson listens as Anderton tells her the European Union has put a billion euros into neuroscience research. It's to create a simulation of the workings of the entire brain. 'Bollocks to that,' she says. 'It's pointless, and creepy.' To her surprise, he agrees. She wonders whether the EU's one-to-one scale map of the brain will actually be a brain. Would it have addiction circuits, like a human brain? And if you prodded them, would it become addicted to, say, mathematical equations, or the *Harvard Law Review*, or browsing Google Earth? And the question of a brain simulation that is actually a brain is so mind-bendingly tricky – probably for the brain-mappers and certainly for her – that she pours herself another tumblerful of vodka and tonic.

She started drinking more after Ben's accident. That was the key moment. She often has flashbacks to seeing him in hospital, all the wires and tubes, the swelling, grotesque stuff. She remembers how he was when he was convalescing. How hard it was to cope with his mood swings. 'Labile,' the doctors called him. He'd always been so easy before, so good-humoured, her Ben. But now he'd fly into rages at the slightest provocation. Or no provocation at all. There was that time she took in his scrambled eggs slightly underdone, or overcooked.

He shouted at her, 'You're fucking useless, that's not how I like them, take it away! Christ, do I have to do everything for myself now?'

She knew she should wait for the thunder in the brain to pass but she couldn't, she was too hurt and offended. 'You have pretty much everything done for you, actually,' she said, and her own words seemed to stoke her anger and she added, 'You're being a bit of an ungrateful little bastard after what I've done for you.'

'Yes, you're my mother, big deal.'

'Ben, I'm sick of this!' She stormed from the room with his tray of food and banged the door shut behind her, and threw the tray onto the hallway floor. Then she went to her room and screamed into a pillow. She cried, bitter and angry with herself. She poured herself a vodka, gulped it neat, went to the kitchen to find the mop and bucket and disinfectant floor cleaner to clear up the mess she'd made. Later, she peered round the door. Ben had calmed down. He smiled at her. He didn't exactly apologise, though. Nor did she.

Months later he did apologise, when she reminded him what it was like looking after him in the early days following the operation. He said, 'I felt like

I was trapped in a stranger's body, like it didn't belong to me, but I couldn't get out of it, it made me so angry. I'm sorry, Mum, it must have been horrendous, me being such a dick.'

'Yes, it was.'

'I think I'll go out with the skateboard today.'

'Don't be an idiot.'

She remembers him grinning, her smiling back and saying, 'Oh, son of mine,' and rubbing his hand. And sitting in the chair reading, while he fell asleep.

These days it's Nick who drives her to drink. She hates him for being so fat, loathes how he looks, worries about him. She knows his colleagues are now hinting that his weight is interfering with his work, though she's not sure how. Perhaps the job is more physically demanding than she imagines. All that concentration must be tiring; she finds it hard to concentrate for five minutes. Perhaps your blood sugar goes up and down too much if you're fat, or your blood pressure's too high, and that affects your clinical judgement. Maybe he's got that Type 2 diabetes. She can't get him to talk about such things, but she's sure he worries about them.

Music of the
hemispheres

Anderton took his eyes from the operating micro-scope, one hand still holding the grip of the surgical micro-scissors, and looked round. He growled his displeasure. Who had inserted that mindless boy-band pap into the soundtrack? Bhattacharya, the anaesthetist, monitoring his screens, raised his eye-brows. The nurses, the registrar, the trainee looked at each other and shrugged. Was that a grin of complici-ty in the far corner, a near-silent snigger to his right?

'Justin Bieber,' said Jenna, the scrub nurse. 'About time we had some decent music.'

'What the hell!' Anderton shouted.

Jenna looked down, stifling a smile.

'I'm not operating to this rubbish. Change it. Somebody change it. Now.'

The track was changed, tranquillity and order were restored. The operation resumed.

During surgery, music was important to An-derton. He didn't have a deep understanding of classical composers, but he liked the effect they produced in him. His colleague Nash would have been scornful of his incoherent musical tastes, like those pedants who insisted you could be a Mozart man or a Beethoven man, not both. As stupid, to Anderton's mind, as insisting you could either be a sophisticated gourmet or a lover of junk food; he was both. So it was with music. He chose different pieces only for their ability to shape his moods and states of mind. He believed that the rhythms, melodies and harmonies helped to activate the parts of his brain where the complex motor repertoires were stored, the moves a surgeon makes.

For a long and difficult operation, he'd oversee the playlist with nearly as much care as he put into planning the procedure itself. In the early stages of cutting through the scalp, drilling bone flaps, incising and folding back the layers of the dura (which he left to his registrar in any case), he was happy to allow upbeat classical music – the allegro of a Haydn symphony, say, or a Beethoven piano concerto. Or even something more 'popular' and to the tastes of his younger colleagues, early Dylan, Bowie.

But once the brain was exposed, he took back musical control. For the long middle stretches, as he tiptoed his way towards the target through the twisting paths of sulci and fissures and ventricles, around the strewn obstacles of critical nerves and arteries, he'd play Bach, something austere yet dynamic and uplifting to maintain his stamina for the long haul. When he reached the seat of the problem, the theatre of war as he thought of it – the minefield of a tangled arteriovenous malformation, or an aneurysm that had to be surgically clipped deep in the brain – he'd choose something that evoked concentrated rigour: a late Beethoven string quartet, for instance.

If the operation was complicated but not especially dangerous, he might have Indian ragas. He enjoyed seeing Bhattacharya's discomfort and irritation when the droning sound of the sitar reached him above the sucking of the pumps and the bleeping of monitors. Bhattacharya would complain that, with raga music, nothing much happened for an inordinately long period, then for no apparent reason it stopped.

Pranab Bhattacharya was third-generation British, born in Edgbaston, educated at the University of Newcastle. He was a fastidious man, precise and measured in everything he did, whereas Anderton could be cavalier, depart from the script, react ingeniously to the unexpected. Anderton suspected that Pranab disapproved of this quality. Though not as much as he disapproved of his colleague's expanding bulk. He was too circumspect to say anything. But there was that twitch of the mouth, that flicker of an eyelid that appeared whenever Anderton groaned at the pains in his shoulder or his knees, or when he fiddled with the adjustable arms of the surgical chair so that it could accommodate him without chafing.

Other colleagues were more pointed in their comments these days. He attempted to ignore them, but he'd been shaken not so long ago by an overheard conversation: two youngsters in the alcove of the neurosurgeons' lounge, the junior trainee and a female medical student on rotation; both insufferable. Their voices, high and excited, amid the clattering of cups and the clinking of spoons as they made coffee. They hadn't heard him come in. He was light on his feet, for a big man. 'It's all that creeping round brothels you do,' Alyson had said once; joking, probably. Even now, his weight over 120 kilos, he could still slip about the place with a certain hefty stealth. Anderton heard the student say, 'What! Prof Anderton? And Jenna? The scrub nurse?'

'Yep,' said the trainee. 'After the departmental drinks party, a few years ago.'

'Wow. She's quite hot.'

'Yeah, I guess. Wouldn't fight her off.'

'Listen to you!'

Anderton stopped in mid-step, straining to catch the rest of the exchange.

'Jesus,' said the junior. 'Like being shagged by a fucking elephant seal.'

The young woman laughed, a silly, ingratiating noise. 'How would you know?'

'On an isolated shore, on a remote island in the South Atlantic, thousands of elephant seals gather to mate. A massive bull asserts his shagging rights over every female in sight...' the trainee declaimed in breathy tones.

She giggled. 'Don't! That's horrid!'

'I mean,' he said, 'at what point do you become too fat to shag?'

'And how, you know, how does he get close enough to actually...?'

'Retractors?'

'No! Don't!'

'If I needed brain surgery, I certainly wouldn't want his fat fingers inside my skull.'

'They're not that fat, strangely.'

'Even so.'

Anderton had crept from the room to the sound of more giggling, vowing to overwhelm the pair of them with mind-numbing administrative jobs and set them to suture cadavers till they threw up.

*

Now, in theatre, as Ravi Shankar and Ali Akbar Khan began to play a raga called 'Bangla Dhun', Anderton said, without looking up from the eye-piece of the operating microscope, 'Thought it was about time you were educated in your cultural heritage, Bhattacharya.'

Particularly in the early days of their partner-ship, Bhattacharya could be an easy victim, quick to bristle. His reaction would lead Anderton's then registrar, the young and unctuous Jamie Boxall, to prick up his ears at the arousing prospect of tension in the operating theatre.

Now Bhattacharya said, 'My cultural heritage,

Nick, is Electric Light Orchestra and Duran Duran and UB40. "Ghost Town" and all that.'

Anderton looked up from his eyepiece. 'Each to his own, just as long as it never comes into theatre.'

'As you know, my musical tastes are Catholic...'

'Catholic, eh? And you a Brummie Brahmin.'

Bhattacharya smiled to himself, scanning the monitors. After a moment he said, 'Incidentally, if you do have to play that tiresome raga stuff, please don't go for Ravi Shankar, an overrated westernised hack beloved of The Beatles and despised in India. Try someone classy, like Nikhil Banerjee.'

'Pleased to see you keep up with what's happening back home.'

'If by back home you mean Birmingham, yes, of course. If you are referring to the Indian subcontinent, well, one keeps oneself informed about the world around one, not just the microcosm of one's narrow professional life. Which in the case of a neurosurgeon is the inside of a dark bone box, is it not?'

There was an intake of breath, the other colleagues turned as one to witness Anderton's reaction. But he merely nodded. 'Touché, Bhattacharya, touché! CO_2 levels OK?'

'CO_2 levels fine,' said Bhattacharya.

'And a very happy Diwali to you too!'

And thus, with sarcasm, banter and music, they maintained their concentration levels through the long reaches of their surgical journey. Though he enjoyed the jousting with Bhattacharya, Anderton in reality loved raga music for the way it got him, as his younger colleagues would say, 'in the zone', a space of intense, relaxed alertness, the music's rhythms seeming to move the fingers with a certainty and grace that in day-to-day life were elusive. Sometimes, when he was fatigued, he would focus on the tabla beat for a minute or two, marvelling at its unpredictable yet inevitable complexities, and this would allow a part of his conscious mind to refresh itself, even as his hands continued their delicate work.

Occasionally, he'd relax his hostility to 'youth music', as he called it. His children had introduced him to a track called 'Green Gloves', and for him it became a defiant anthem, to be played in the home stretches of particularly complex procedures requiring repeated, dangerous small moves. The song, with its insistent beat, seemed to fit the rhythm of his micro-movements, whatever speed he was working at. It buoyed him up and swept him along without rushing him, and as his sugar levels dropped towards the end of a long operation, it energised him. And the song's lyrics amused him, with their talk of slipping oneself into other people's skulls – which was after all what a neurosurgeon did.

But there was another, sourer layer of meaning. On bleak days, the words about watching their videos and loving their loves seemed to proclaim the way his obesity made him an observer of the lives of other people. He was, when it came down to it, a voyeur. The possibilities of the physical world were shrinking as he expanded. A year or so before, he'd realised that his feet no longer fitted into his old shoes. Another humiliation to assimilate: he was not just a fat man, but fat-footed too. His sex life had become non-existent, even in his fantasies. Soon the prospect loomed of degenerating into a stuffing-shitting beast, unable even to reach round the surfaces of his own body to wipe his arse. He'd already reached the point where the adjustable armrests on his surgical chair were, even fully extended, too tight around his flanks. The bulges round his waist were growing their own bulges. Presumably, manufacturers of theatre equipment did not cater to the outsized gentleman surgeon. What would happen when the physical limits were reached? Operating was now the only thing, other than eating, that gave him a sense of purpose and identity, and if he continued to gain weight, he'd sooner or later be unable to continue.

In such moods, he'd ban 'Green Gloves' from operations until he felt less bad about the world.

There was one piece of music, however, that he never tolerated: Mozart's Clarinet Concerto. Just seeing the title, in the music section of a newspaper, say, could provoke a sick wrenching in his guts. If he happened to hear snatches of it on an automated telephone answering system, or while flicking through stations on his car radio, he'd end the phone call or turn off the radio. Even a number plate containing the string K622 could upset him.

For the music was tainted by association with a surgical disaster. The small details of that day, the things you'd normally pay no attention to, were branded into his mind. The smells of the disinfectant. The anxious expression of the anaesthetist. The tense murmured calls for more units of blood. The scrub nurse's fumbling for the correct suction tip. And the music playing: Mozart's Clarinet Concerto in A, K. 622, so light and clean and upbeat, so blameless and now so contaminated, so darkened by tragedy. The disaster had shattered him and, several years on, the memory of it still disturbed his sleep, upset his equanimity, strained his relationships. It had provided the 'big bang' that set him on the path from robustly overweight to compulsively obese.

So the clarinet concerto was banned from the operating theatre. As was, to be on the safe side, the whole of the Mozart canon. Bhattacharya, a Mozart aficionado, would have loved to carry out his work to the accompaniment of the piano concertos, or the operas. But he'd been present at the disaster, and though he had nothing to reproach himself for, he understood and accepted the prohibition. He understood, above all, that Anderton needed to follow his own advice to students: you will kill people, always go forwards, never backwards. The surgeon dared not peer behind him for fear that, like Lot's wife, he'd be transformed into a pillar of salt.

Alyson

Alyson has been caught on the hop. Sophie has just told her that plenty of women use them these days.

'Stop it,' says Alyson. 'I'm your mother.'

'You should try it, Mum. Surprise yourself.' Many of her friends have them, so she says.

Alyson thinks, You wouldn't talk to your father like that. But perhaps that isn't true. Sophie and Nick have this father–daughter thing going. Especially since Ben's little episode. She thinks of her children's growing-up in terms of *before* and *after* Ben's little episode, which wasn't so little. What is it, eight, nine years ago now? Amazing how time passes. Somehow Nick doesn't seem to infuriate Sophie the way Alyson does, and he stays calm while she's all spit and fury. So maybe they do natter away, the pair of them, about sex toys and periods and…

'I thought old people these days were supposed to think about sex all the time,' says Sophie.

'I'm not old.'

'For God's sake, Mum, it's like going for a good shit or having your nails done in a nail bar!'

And in pretty much the same emotional register, thinks Alyson.

'You just go and knock out a quick one, no big deal.'

'Sophie! Stop! I'm not prepared to have this conversation.' Cosy mother–daughter chit-chat is what she wants, not hen-party banter. She shudders. She will not resort to one of those things. She'd rather explode, and the way things are going, it could come to that.

God, what would her parents have made of the idea? Did they even *have* sex? More than the twice, once for her and once for her sister? She can't imagine it. Her father Gerald was so staid and dull. Wore his hair combed back, slicked with hair cream; she can almost smell it, a mix of sickly sweet brilliantine and waxy hair odour. Christ, did they still use that stuff in the seventies? Her father did, unless she's misremembering. Maybe he bought in stocks to last, back in the fifties. He used to travel to work in central London, from the end of the Piccadilly line, in a dark blue suit and with a rolled umbrella. Man of habit. Liked regularity. She can still visualise the large tub of Senokot on the bathroom shelf. He collected stamps. Her mother always called him Gerald, never Gerry. He called her Irene or, when he was attempting to be jovial, Rene. She had lacquered brown hair, fire risk. Frustrated eyes. Had never worked, always wore a skirt, wouldn't have worn trousers in case people made comments about her husband. She had a friend called Janet who went with her once a week to the Gaumont Cinema. They saw *Grease, Close Encounters, The Stud, Star Wars*. She would come back humming the *Star Wars* theme, or 'You're the One That I Want'. Not when Gerald was around, he liked peace and quiet. She kept a bottle of whiskey behind her dressing table that he didn't know about. But Alyson did.

She remembers that her father did a very boring job. Some kind of accountant. No, not accountant. Actuary. That was it, actuary. His only attempt at humour was when people at parties asked him what he did for a living: 'I'm an actuary, actually.' And he'd give a brief honk of a laugh. At those parties her mother would fortify herself and be bright and laugh too much and talk too loudly and fall into a gloom by bedtime and stay in bed in the dark the next day with a 'migraine', while her father sat in the dining room attaching small hinges to postage stamps from the British colonies and crown dependencies and, after consulting his Stanley Gibbons catalogue, stuck them in albums. The biggest excitement of his life came the day he discovered a rare colour variant of a 25c Sarawak stamp depicting Rajah Brooke, the white rajah. 'It's not even in Stanley Gibbons!' he cried. 'I'll go and put the beef in the oven,' said Irene. Alyson understood, even as a kid, that it was her mother's chance to get away from him and have a tipple in peace. By the time she escaped to university, she knew how her mother felt.

Alyson's father tried, without success, to interest his girls in the stamp collection. They preferred to go down the garden to the garage where the big Volvo was kept and play doctors and nurses with the two wild boys next door.

She's often constipated these days, perhaps a tub of Senokot would be a good investment. At least she's not putting on weight. Nick thinks she doesn't know about the wrappers for family-sized chocolate bars that he's stuffed in the bin, or about his secret stash in the bottom drawer of the desk in his study. He locks it, but leaves the key in the pot on the desktop. So perhaps he really wants her to discover his secret. Anyway, she's sneaked a look. Inside, she found – apart from a locked cash box she's still curious about – neat stacks of chocolate bars. There's Boosts, Snickers, Double Deckers; two cylinders of Pringles; a large paper bag filled with assorted liquorice pieces; a jumbo packet of cashews, open and secured with an elastic band (which at least means he didn't finish the bag at one sitting – or perhaps he was disturbed in flagrante). He apparently thinks she hasn't seen the inexpertly brushed-away crisp fragments on the floor, thinks she doesn't notice the tiny biscuit crumbs between the sheets on his bed.

At least these days, he seems to realise that when other women look at him, they're gawping at the spectacle, not eyeing him up. She's watched them watching him as he goes round the supermarket aisles for the weekly shop. She can almost hear the collective tut-tutting when he takes down large pork pies by the half dozen, or party packs of cheese-and-onion crisps, or tins of chocolate-coated biscuits, or litres of ice cream (he's fond of Cornetto). He pretends not to notice the censorious looks. Sometimes she'll say, 'Do we really need six of those?' and he'll respond, 'They've a long shelf life, no harm in stocking up.' But he's not stocking up, he's consuming. She can't bear seeing him self-destruct, she plans to tell him to do the shopping on his own.

False-belief errors

It was a fine late-spring morning as Anderton made his way from the hospital to the medical school to deliver one of his lectures to third-year students. He descended to the basement clinging to the handrail. Going down was worse than coming up: there was always the anticipation of the sharp pain deep within the knee, and the feeling that the leg would wobble sideways and give way. The anticipation was worse than the pain itself. He braced his foot carefully with each step, until his ankle joints ached too. Students and staff coming up the stairs squeezed in and made themselves small to give him room. In the basement, he moved along the corridor with little shuffling steps, barely raising his feet; it was pointless to lift more weight than he had to.

He entered the steeply tiered lecture theatre and sat on the desk at the front, one leg resting against the floor, arms folded; a glass of water within reach. Soon the future doctors filed in, expectant and attentive, for his lectures were popular. They started on time and latecomers were not admitted.

Students thought he was a bit of 'a legend'. They'd even created a page on social media devoted to his pronouncements. 'Satyriasis: nature's neurological cock-up'; or 'The worst smell in neurosurgery? The smell of failure'. That sort of thing: not terribly witty, somewhat brutal. Anderton supposed the students went round repeating his *bons mots*, imitating his droll, emphatic intonation. He spoke these days seated at the lecture theatre desk, unable to stand for long periods. His immobility, accompanied by small, precise hand gestures, intensified the fascination he exerted over his audience.

He began today's lecture as always by explaining that surgeons have to tread a fine line between arrogance and humility. The under-confident, too-humble practitioner is likely to be tense and tentative. The hand may shake and, with margins for error in neurosurgery measured in fractions of millimetres, this may prove fatal. But overconfidence is also to be avoided. You fly too close to the sun, your wings melt, you plummet. He warned them of these dangers while aware of his own tendencies towards arrogance. It had been his undoing in the past.

He continued, with minimal notes, looking up often at the ranks of faces. Occasionally he lifted his glasses to his forehead and fixed his eyes on some timid individual in one of the lower tiers, *pour encourager les autres*. He moved towards the heart of the matter: the strictest logic, the most caring personality, the most sublime technical skill could not save you from disaster if your initial premise was wrong. He called this category of mistake 'false-belief error', and insisted that it was the most dangerous type, because it was so insidious and so hard to guard against.

In patients, wrong beliefs sometimes resulted from brain injury or disease, as with Cotard's syndrome. Here he paused to ask a student to explain for the benefit of the others what Cotard's syndrome was. When the poor victim failed, he said, 'It's a neurological condition in which you are convinced (inaccurately) that you are dead. Or, alternatively, immortal but without a soul. And nobody can persuade you otherwise.'

Of course, similar false-belief errors were common in everyday life. Sometimes they were merely embarrassing, as when you chatted to a guest at a party under the impression he or she was someone else entirely. On other occasions they might be fatal: you stepped off a kerb sure that the traffic was coming from the right, whereas in fact you were in a one-way street and it was coming from the left.

As Anderton talked, a young woman in the centre of the front row stood up to recover a dropped pen. She blushed slightly and pushed her long, straight dark hair away from her face as she bent down, glancing nervously at Anderton. He caught a waft of her perfume, dense and obscure. He experienced a queer dizzying feeling, like standing at the edge of a void. He lost his train of thought for a moment. The students seemed anxious on his behalf. He took a sip from the glass of water on his desk and scanned his sheet of notes. He found the next point he wanted to cover, and when he put down the glass the world seemed still, and normal again.

In neurosurgeons, he explained, false-belief syndrome affected the arrogant along with the too-cautious or the self-doubting. And it was sometimes disastrous for the patient. He cited the case of a respected surgeon who'd operated on a patient in the false belief that she had a left-sided glioma. He dug around in her left hemisphere for quite a while without finding the tumour. In the process he destroyed her language centre. It turned out that the glioma had been on the right side of the brain all along, and there it remained. She was left unable to understand or utter speech. The surgeon had been so fixed in his wrong belief that he was operating on the correct hemisphere of the brain that even reviewing the notes and the scans beforehand did not shake that belief. There'd been some confusion with a patient of a similar name. It was an unlikely chain of circumstances, but given how many operations are performed, bound to happen.

How to prevent such things? Well, said Anderton, in this case there were checks, and they failed. The surgeon assumed that anomalies in the patient's notes were down to clerical error. A nurse pointed out that the scan appeared to be displayed back to front. She was ignored, because there is a hierarchy in operating theatres and nurses are not near the top of it; she knew better than to insist.

A hum of disapproval rose in the lecture hall, and Anderton paused, held up his hand for silence. 'But,' he said, 'such hierarchy is necessary for good order.' Another murmur in the hall. 'Therefore,' he continued, 'we have a conundrum. If you're too respectful of a surgeon's judgement, people will die because of his or her false beliefs. On the other hand, if a surgeon's judgement can be challenged, people will die because of the lack of order in theatre, where a complex operation needs to be conducted like a military campaign, and so needs a clear line of command.'

He came to his concluding lesson. 'Surgeons are human, even neurosurgeons. Human beings make errors. They grasp the wrong end of the stick and don't let go of it. Good systems can mitigate errors only up to a point. People will die. Get used to it.' Anderton always enjoyed the sight of his students' disillusioned faces at this point in the lecture, as they took in the dashing of their aspirations to help humanity.

But after the lecture, he still felt uneasy at his momentary stumble earlier, his glimpse into the void, triggered by the smell of the young woman's perfume. What did it mean? He struggled to remember. It wasn't related to his own defining Icarus moment – that was a looming presence always, however much he tried to blot it out. No, this had been something else.

As he drove home, the memory finally surfaced, like a body floating up from the lake. It was not so much traumatic as embarrassing, a false-be-lief, wrong-end-of-the-stick error, damaging to his vanity and sense of self; nobody died. Paris, autumn 2010, or was it 2011? The hospital of La Pitié-Salpêtrière.

Back then, Anderton was already a big man, well on the way to becoming a *fat* man, but not as fat as now. He still tried to dress well, possibly a little stylish for a neurosurgeon, and had a careful-ly trimmed moustache and goatee, sandy blond in colour. His kids, who mocked his facial hair for its pretensions, would have been late teens: Ben stu-dious, sporty and upbeat, Sophie a year older, still awkward and prone to bouts of verbal aggression; his wife Alyson still just about handsome in her pared-down way, already drinking too much.

The head of neurosurgery at La Pitié-Salpêtrière had invited Anderton to Paris where he talked to col-leagues about the innovative tweaks in brain cancer surgery being developed in London, and addressed a colloquium. He showed slides and videos of his oper-ations. The holy grail, he said, was a reliable method of distinguishing cancerous from healthy tissue. This would allow surgeons to avoid false-belief errors, in which they routinely missed the malignant parts of the brain and cut out the good parts. In the meantime, there were small improvements to be made. As a junior doctor some two decades before, he'd done a medical internship in Montreal, and spoke fluent French. He had an extensive medical vocabulary and an atrocious accent. When he spoke the language, he overlaid the peculiar, lilting Québecois rhythms and drawled vowels with an incorrigible English accent. Parisian colleagues found the performance grotesque but amusing, like a dancing bear, and so subtly encouraged him. The talk went well, the audience engaged by his flamboyant, outsized presence.

Anderton's attention had been drawn to a disconcertingly attractive delegate from a department of neurosurgery in Lyons. Her name was Marie-Laure Lavigne. She'd sat through the sessions quietly, intervening from time to time to make perceptive, serious comments in a low voice. She was not so much pretty, reckoned Anderton, as nicely put together, elegant when in motion, with an olive complexion, taut skin, well groomed. She had a high cheek-boned, sulky aura to her. When Anderton was responding in his fluently hideous French to a question from one of the neurosurgeons, Marie-Laure raised her fine hazel eyes and looked at him, both furtive and shameless he thought, and his insides twisted and he knew, he just knew... Or believed he did.

After the final session, he joined delegates for a long lunch of several courses: seafood, entrecôte of beef, rare regional cheeses, liqueur-laced dessert, several glasses of fine wine, and the mandatory digestif. He was pleased to learn that Marie-Laure would be with them for farewell snacks and drinks and further networking that evening at the Club de Luxembourg in the 16th arrondissement.

Anderton returned to his hotel near Les Invalides for a siesta and to prepare for the evening. Any guilt he felt was swept away by the prospect of the chase and the slow-building erotic tension.

*

That evening, things could not have got off to a better start. Anderton had manoeuvred himself to sit opposite Marie-Laure at the end of the long dining table. On her left was a hospital administrator who swiped endlessly at his mobile phone and paid no attention to her, or anyone else. Next to Anderton was a Korean neurologist, talking loudly to his Korean neighbour in their own language. So Anderton and Marie-Laure were in a kind of bubble, while the murmur of speech and clatter of cutlery went on around them. They talked. Mainly, he talked, and she lifted her unsettling eyes to him every so often.

'I thought your contribution was *brillante*,' she said.

He nodded. 'Thank you. Your own interventions were acute and to the point.'

She gave the hint of a smile. 'And how was your afternoon?'

58

'Interesting, if you will permit me a small anecdote.' He pronounced 'anecdote' as if talking English. She seemed charmed by this.

'Of course,' she said, 'please go ahead.'

'Perhaps we could address each other as *tu* – would that disturb you?'

'If you wish,' she said, still using the formal *vous*. He should probably have taken this as a warning sign, but in his excitement he barely noticed. 'This afternoon,' he said, 'a rather curious thing happened to me.'

'Oh?'

'Yes. After a very good lunch, I returned to my hotel to take a nap. But when I went back to my room and got into bed, the sheets *stank*. Incredible, no? So I gave up on the nap and went down to reception to complain. I made the manager pass a bad quarter of an hour, I can tell you!'

Marie-Laure was smiling, he had her attention. He took a sip of wine and continued. 'The fellow says, "But monsieur, our sheets here are clean, this is a hotel of the highest category!" I insisted and, of course, he gave way, and they changed the bed linen. The chance of sleep had gone, so I ordered a coffee in the lounge. And, believe it or not, the smell was still there!'

Marie-Laure laughed. She sounded a little tentative. But Anderton was encouraged.

'So,' he continued. 'It was following me around like... like a lost dog.' He felt pleased at his poetic metaphor. 'Unbelievable, no?' He wound himself up for the dramatic denouement. 'And do you know what, the smell was coming from *me*! From my moustache to be precise.'

'My God,' said Marie-Laure, throwing her hand to her mouth and laughing again, more naturally this time.

'I couldn't work it out. Then I remembered the lunch.'

'The lunch? How the lunch?'

'The cheese course. I'd eaten a selection of cheeses, including a spectacularly ripe Époisses de Bourgogne, so soft it was practically vibrating. Anyway, I went to the washroom, washed my moustache, and *voilà*, the smell was gone!'

Marie-Laure seemed fully engaged in the tale. Perhaps she admired the way this eminent neurosurgeon could tell stories against himself. She said, 'So, an unfortunate case of *Brevibacterium*.'

'Indeed.'

There was a glowing sense of amused complicity. They'd been so locked together in their communion that it was only now that Anderton noticed the Korean neighbour to his right had been supplanted by a distinguished-looking older woman, as uninterested in him as the previous individual.

'And did you tell the hotel of your mistake?' Marie-Laure asked, forgetting for the first time to use *vous*.

'No,' said Anderton. He thought he'd told the

story well, revealed quite cunningly his attractive little weakness. 'No, Marie-Laure,' he said. 'I was far too ashamed!'

She laughed, he laughed, her foot brushed his by accident – or not – beneath the table. She raised her arms as if to say, *Oh-là-là*! The abrupt movement must have sent a wave of volatile compounds in his direction, because he caught her perfume, something edgy and dark, with tones of soil and fresh-cut fungi and musk. Her smile was so intimate he felt bold enough to say, 'I hope you don't find me impolite, or worse, but may I ask what scent you're wearing? It's very distinctive.'

'Oh, that. It's nothing. I don't even remember,' she said airily. 'Oh yes, Poison, I think. Something like that, something pretentious. My mother gave it to me as a present.' She shook her head with a look of cynical amusement. 'Rather a curious gift from a mother to a daughter, *n'est-ce pas*? What was she trying to tell me, exactly?'

In the light from the tall, fat candles in the silver candelabra, her eyes sparkled. Anderton drank more wine, raised his glass to her, experiencing a delightful sense of oneness with this younger woman, of the two of them against the mediocre world. This was more than mere lust, it was on a higher plane. Though, yes, lust was definitely there. Marie-Laure twiddled with her ear stud. The effect on Anderton was almost unbearably erotic. What did she see in him, he wondered. A certain mastery of his field, his way of being in the world? His knowledge, wisdom, *savoir-faire*? Perhaps his physical presence – not handsome exactly, but reassuring, hefty, solid; someone whose sturdy arms a woman would wish to feel protecting and comforting her.

She said, 'Do you believe in matches made in heaven?'

'I'm sure they exist,' he said, as he stared into her hazel eyes.

'I think I've met him, met my match.' There was a moment's stillness, like smoke hanging in the air. Anderton could hardly breathe as he prayed to no particular god that he should not have a coronary infarct sitting there at the table, not now, not in this sublime space and moment. He refilled his glass, and hers.

'What's his name?' he whispered. Her eyes had a misted look, her lips were parted.

'Thomas,' she said. 'Thomas Bellegarde. *Gastroentérologue.*' She smiled inwardly.

He felt the hot and cold of embarrassment, shame, a middle-aged man's foolishness. He should have known better. He'd grasped the wrong end of the stick.

'Good,' he managed to say. 'Excellent. I congratulate you. Young love, and so on.'

'Thank you!'

He muttered, through dry lips, 'Should we try the cured ham, I heard somebody saying it was particularly good.'

'Not for me, thanks.' She smiled politely, a bit distant now.

'Or that old blue cheese?'

'Oh no, it's a bit old and blue for me.' She looked at him steadily. Was that a hint of irony in her eyes, or even mockery?

Soon Anderton was getting to his feet, saying his farewells with formal courtesy, shaking Marie-Laure's hand, wishing her luck in life, in her career, using the formal *vous* again, as she did to him. *Fool*, he thought as he walked out into the sharp autumnal air of the rue Foucault, *fool, bloody fool, bloody fat middle-aged fool*.

*

Anderton reflected, as he finished the journey back from the medical school, turning the Mercedes into secluded, tree-lined Horsley Avenue, that the Paris incident had been some kind of critical point in his life and career. Sure, he'd made a fool of himself. The Frenchwoman had manipulated him, led him *by the fucking dick*, as Alyson would have put it. But Paris was worse than that. It was the moment perception caught up with reality. For too long, a part of his brain had tricked him into believing himself to be the Anderton of old: imposing, heavyset, 'big-boned', sexually vigorous, attractive to women. After Paris, he was forced to recognise that his new reality was as a fat man, to accept that no woman would see him and fantasise about – let alone consent to – a quick, illicit coupling. Shorn of self-delusion, he now had only eating to fall back on, to give him relief from the misery of self-knowledge.

He drove under the canopies of the chestnut trees, their candles just about to flower. The sun flashed intermittently between the leaves and, trying to adjust his eyes to the rapidly changing light, he had a vision of his childhood self: the chubby boy of the class at primary, too bright and bored to knuckle down, then the shock of the local secondary school where PE classes became a torment. The changing rooms rang with the bullies' gross laughter. They would shout out in gym, 'Sir, Anderton's getting titties, sir!', the girls jeering along with the boys. Nobody picked him for their team: he was adept on the ball, but he had no puff, and wasn't cool. He'd be miserable, silent, taking refuge in solitary pursuits, studying maths and biology books, or endlessly playing a little video game in which a chicken ran to catch eggs in a basket before they hit the ground. And eating, always eating. He took to school a plastic lunch box filled with salty blood pudding and bacon sandwiches, the produce of his father's shop. The congealed pig fat against the soft white bread seemed lusciously consoling to him. After school, he'd sneak up to his room to raid his hoard of fizzy cola sweets, candy canes, fruit pastilles (his mouth watered even now at the memory of the blackcurrant flavour, sweet and intense), and the jelly babies that for some reason he always ate head first. At night, he might raid the freezer for a surreptitious Cornetto. He grew fatter still. His father would say, 'Don't pay them any heed, Nicholas, I was like that at your age, a big lad, grew out of it, didn't I. It's a family thing.' He *had* grown out of it, as his father had predicted. He'd reached fifteen, hormones had kicked in, he'd put on a growth spurt, solidified, and the fat had mostly turned to muscle. He could outplay his former taunters on the football pitch, and the girls who'd been mocking started to sidle up to him and flirt.

Anderton's father, Alf, had always helped him through the tough times, encouraged him, hadn't judged him. Alf was a high-class butcher, 'Purveyor of Fine Meats to Discerning Customers', as the lettering on the window read. A driven man, energetic and uneducated, but loving, he had started out in south-east London. As he prospered, he moved west and north away from Forest Hill. He ended up beyond the North Circular Road in a pre-war semi-detached in Pinner, a five-minute walk from his butcher's premises in the parade of shops on the high street. As a boy, Anderton would go through to the back of the shop where the meat hung. His father would be standing in his bloodied butcher's apron at a thick wooden table, sunken in the middle through use and scored with an infinity of marks of knives and cleavers. He'd be quartering lamb carcases or hacking at sides of beef with violent precision. He had long, slender fingers, the hands of a pianist or a surgeon, as Anderton came to think in later years. What he loved most was seeing his father pluck and gut chickens, one after the other, in a hypnotic dance of hands. The glistening entrails tugged out and slithering into a large bucket, the chopped-off heads into another bin, the livers, gizzards and hearts into an enamelled white bowl. That blood-rust smell. The blinding speed of the movements, like a martial artist's. He would stay there entranced until his father, looking up, told him to go and study, do his homework. 'Don't be an ignoramus like your father, Nicholas,' he'd say in an accent that had lost some of its flat South London vigour. The boy would reply, 'I'm going to be a surgeon when I grow up, Dad.' 'Good for you, son, good for you.' Chop, pluck, pull, slither, plop, chop...

*

As he came to a halt and parked on the gravel drive-way of the modish, architect-designed house, with its rectangular tower of wood and glass, he thought that he'd have to watch out for the pigeons. At this time of year, their frenetic mating rites seemed to loosen their bowels. It wouldn't do the car's paintwork any good. Their shit formed thickened guanoesque deposits that hardened in the sun, and he wouldn't be able to scrape them off, because he could not lift his arm above shoulder height without the pain of inflamed tendons and the grind of the under-lubricated joint. He'd have to take the car, probably weekly over the summer, to the car wash.

Anderton got out of the Mercedes, clutching his briefcase and the discarded wrappers of milk chocolate bars. He entered the house and, with rasping breaths, climbed the stairs to the bathroom and sat down to piss; he could no longer safely urinate standing up, because there was no clear line of sight. Reaching down, he wiped the drips, and got off the toilet. He examined himself in the mirror, seeing the neat imprint of the seatbelt's webbing on the under-hang of his belly. He'd have to rub in emollient and zinc cream to prevent the chapping, moist flesh from breeding fungal infestations. And, with self-disgust, he observed the swelling flap of pubic fat below the belly. It seemed to be slowly engulfing his sexual organ, like some medicine man's curse. At this rate, in a year or two he'd be suffering from full-blown *buried penis syndrome*, the literal retreat of his manhood. For every additional two or three stone of excess weight he'd lose a further inch of visible penis, buried in fat. He'd then face the prospect of pooling urine, infection, odours, and uncertain surgery to repair the damage: skin grafts to the shaft, surgical lipectomy, reduction scrotoplasty. The hazily-remembered routine of the sexual act surfaced in his mind, of Organ A slotting into Organ B. But without the aid of a mirror, he was hardly sure where Organ A was. These days, with the weight of his gut crushing the thousands of delicate nerve endings of his genitalia, he felt little desire; and what he thought was desire was the memory of it, which shimmered away to nothing.

He well understood the vicious spiral: in compensation for the loss of his sexual persona he ate even more, speeding the burial of his former pleasures, marking the site with a sarcophagus of fat.

Alyson

Alyson is dealing with a complicated case at the moment, working on it at home. It involves conflicting legal principles. When she was young, she thought the law would be logical, clear, consistent. Beautiful like mathematics is beautiful. But it's not, it comes with layers of stuff, some of it centuries old, statute and case law, and the layers don't fit neatly together. Her current case is particularly messy. She'll have to consult the partners, and knows she'll get different answers from each, and that the bits of advice will be mutually contradictory.

She's going round in circles, she needs a break. The bottle of white wine is in the fridge. She resists for half an hour, but the pressure is building in her head. Not the pressure of the cerebrospinal fluid that Anderton is always banging on about. Another kind of pressure. It's like a relentless mechanical arm squeezing her thoughts until they haven't got space to breathe. A little drink will unsquash her thoughts. She goes to the fridge.

The law is like memory, she thinks. Layer upon

layer. But memory and rigour are at cross purposes. The more precise the memory, the more it resists generalisations. And generalisations are the guts of abstract thought and logic, and of legal theory. She hates the way disorderly reality – all those details, all those bloody facts – contaminates the purity.

Details get in the way. Nick has brain-damaged people in his clinic who can never forget *anything*, so they're overwhelmed by detail. One patient of his couldn't get the idea of a face, just the features of particular faces with countless ways of being distinct from one another. What about the concept of *marriage*? she wonders. Can she grasp what that might mean, or just the unedifying details of her and Nick, a quarter of a century locked in their particular maddening embrace? There's much she can't remember about their lives together, and much of what she can remember she'd rather forget.

She's tried to engage with him many times on all this, on minds and concepts and facts. But he won't respond. He'll say, '"Mind" is a philosophical notion, I leave it to the neuroscientists.'

'Aren't neurosurgeons neuroscientists too?'

'I deal with what's in the box in front of me. Stuff. Stuff you can cut and stitch and suck out.'

When he says that, she thinks about sex.

She's read about the brain: Luria, Sacks, Jakobsen, Damasio. Nick sneers at these people. He says they're playing to the gallery, charlatans, self-publicists, popularisers. She's not sure he's even read them. He doesn't like reading all that much. He likes exploring inside the head. And in expensive restaurants (and cheap ones). And, when he was less obese, in women, other than his wife.

Somebody once wrote: suppose the world was created a few moments ago complete with human beings who hold the memory of a past that never really existed. She thinks about this and concludes that past happiness is an illusion, as if it never happened, but past misery is real, it leaves its footprints on the brain. So in a way the past really is present, in the neurons, that's not just a metaphorical way of speaking. What about her present misery, is it laying down permanent tracks in the brain to plague her in the future? Now she worries about the future. Incontinence, alcoholic dementia. Not a true dementia, Nick says, more alcohol-related brain damage caused by thiamine deficiency – Korsakoff's syndrome. 'Wet brain' it's called. Wet knickers, wet brain, she thinks. *Fuck*! Korsakoff. Course I can't. Course you can. Korsyukan. Korsakoff.

Aequanimitas

At her first consultation, Sandra Grayling had come into Anderton's office with her husband as if auditioning for a talent contest. They were in their late thirties, he lanky and grinning, she with a fat body and thin arms and a nervous, puffy moon face. Anderton consulted his notes and examined her in her underwear. 'She's got the hump, Doctor,' said the husband, amused with himself. So she did: a rounded lump of fat just below the neck. The buffalo hump. And the striations on her belly, the thin skin and the bruising. Cushing's disease.

Now, after tests, the couple had returned to Anderton's office. He thought perhaps he should open his file and, like the compère on a TV talent show, let the tension build before announcing the result.

'The good news is...' he began, and the woman took her husband's hand and squeezed it. 'The good news is that we've identified a small tumour in the pituitary gland at the base of the brain. That's the root of the problem, and we can treat it. The pituitary gland regulates the production of hormones that...'

'And the bad news, Doctor?' asked the woman.

'There is no bad news, other than the fact that treatment will require an operation to remove the tumour. And surgery always carries risk.'

'Like – brain surgery, you mean?'

'Yes.'

'And will it make me lose weight?'

'Over time you should return to something like your normal weight, yes.'

'And this thing?' she asked, pointing to the hump.

'Yes, that should resolve. Over time.'

The husband greeted every remark of Anderton's with a kind of guffaw that was silent but for the hiss of the little puffs of air expelled between his narrow lips. Anderton stared at him, with a professional severity, but it failed to deter him.

'I don't know, Doctor,' he said, eyeing Anderton's bulk. 'Looks like you could do with the operation yourself!'

'This is a serious business, Mr Grayling, we're talking about an operation that's risky. Why do you think your brain is shut up in a sort of strongbox made of solid bone? Because it's not meant to be tampered with. It's a very complicated piece of kit, and once it's exposed to the outside air, potentially—'

'Yeah, but all surgery is risky, isn't it, Doctor? Life is risky, isn't it. That's life.' He resumed his silent laughing while his wife wrung her hands and tried to apologise for him. Anderton felt a flush rise in his cheeks. He'd been put in a bad mood by Grayling's snide jocularity, his allusion to girth, his effortless lack of deference.

*

The surgery was straightforward. Through the hole his registrar had cut in the bone at the top of the nasal passage, Anderton viewed the bony structure, the sella turcica or Turkish saddle, and within it the pituitary gland dangling its two little conjoined sacs on a veiny stalk, like miniature genitalia.

Anderton enjoyed the nomenclature of the brain. The neurosurgical pioneers who'd named the parts would have been hardened professionals of medicine like himself. Yet they'd come across these places and seen shapes in them, like kids seeing dragons in clouds, and the names had an arcane poetry. So, along with the Turkish saddle there was the Sylvian fissure and Meckel's cave; the inferior colliculus and the cingulate gyrus, the optic chiasm and the claustrum, the sulci and the pons, the hippocampus and the fornix and the infundibulum... Having been taught the derivations of the Latin terms in medical school, he'd see before him changing landscapes of ditches and furrows, bridges and aqueducts and vaults, seahorses and funnels, trenches and hillocks.

With the dura snipped and peeled back, the pituitary lay in front of Anderton. Magnified in the binocular eyepieces, the pea-sized organ was glistening and pink. On its underside lay the tiny whitish tumour. Measured against the tip of the forceps, it was about the size of a mustard seed. Even now, as an experienced surgeon, he found it wondrous and strange that something so easily overlooked could have caused this woman's symptoms, led her to put on several stone, thinned her skin till it bruised like a softening pear, heaped fat into a hump between her shoulders. The scale of the cause and the effect seemed out of proportion.

He finished the operation and left his registrar to close up. The patient would be fine. Remove the cause and, with time, you remove the effects. With the words of Grayling in his mind – 'looks like you could do with the operation yourself, Doc!' – he wished his own circumstances were so straightforward. But his obesity had no simple cause. Of course it had a proximate cause: his hyperphagia. The fact that he ate to excess, that he ate despite satiety. He did not care to investigate too deeply the reasons why.

Anderton went to the surgeons' gowning room, trying not to glance at himself in the mirror, but peripherally aware of his shadowy bulk. Perhaps Grayling was right in some sense, in his ignorance. An operation to reduce the size of his stomach would resolve the effect, if not treat the cause. Did that matter? He'd read somewhere, or perhaps his colleague Rabinovich had told him, that after surgery people often found they had more willpower, as if the act of reducing the stomach had an effect on brain chemistry.

He felt that he couldn't go on like this. There was no one thing, just the slow accumulation of incidents. Nash's sarcastic comments on his 'heavyweight contributions'. His patients' sneering, Bhattacharya's raised eyebrow. The recent incident in San Sebastián, of the kite surfer blown through the window, that had triggered in Anderton an obscure but unnerving feeling of finality, like a warning, or an omen. The past humiliations, such as his junior's jibe about mating elephant seals, the fiasco with Marie-Laure in Paris. And always Alyson's scorn, sometimes silent, sometimes vocal.

There were also the health risks. He was well aware of them, of course: the high blood pressure, the diabetes, the heart disease, the strokes, the unpleasant skin infections, the cancers of the alimentary canal, the joints failing, the impotence. Knew them with his intellect, if not with his gut. They worried him on a daily basis, especially when he woke up exhausted after a poor night's sleep because of his obstructed breathing. But what concerned him most was whether he'd still be able to do his job. Or would be allowed to do it.

The previous week, the clinical director had called him in for a meeting and had raised, tactfully enough, the effect of Anderton's obesity on his professional competence. It was a question of finely-balanced judgement, hard calls. There had been murmurings. Concerns. From other staff he was not at liberty to name.

So, thought Anderton, someone had ratted on him. It could have been any of them. From the afore-mentioned Jenna the scrub nurse (though probably not), to his registrar, or that gelled-up nincompoop of a surgical trainee. Or Nash, the other neurosurgical consultant, his rival. Yes, it could well be Nash, damn him. It *had* to be him. He'd have slipped poison into the clinical director's ear:

A fine surgeon, Anderton. Has had the odd clinical disaster, of course, though haven't we all. But I'm a bit concerned at the moment. We must do all we can to help him, given the strain he's under and, erm, the issue of his weight. Neurosurgery, as we know, isn't a matter of sitting down comfortably at your operating microscope. You need to be able to stand, often for long periods. I'm not saying there's a question of fitness to practise. But it's always best to nip these things in the bud. Of course, I'm only really worried about the safety of patients... Blah-blah-blah-blah-blah.

Yes, the rat had to be Nash. Arrogant, aggressive, ambitious Nash. Arsehole.

'Look,' the clinical director had said, 'I'd like you to book a holiday, take paid leave. Have a break. Go to a health spa or whatever. Take up some exercise. Nothing too strenuous. Come back refreshed. In good shape to keep going. And if you decide on the radical solution...'

'What, the surgery?'

'Yes, the surgery.'

'I'm not planning on surgery.'

'I thought you discussed it with Phil Rabinovich.'

'Discussed it. Hypothetically.'

The clinical director sighed. 'Take a holiday, think about it, give yourself some time.'

'I don't want a bloody holiday.'

'Nick, don't box me in.' The clinical director's tone had turned aggressive and impatient. 'You know how this goes.'

Yes, Anderton knew how it went. The next time there was cause for concern, the clinical director would refer him up to the medical director, some mediocre clinician who'd reached (or exceeded) the limits of his competence and gained a new lease of life as a bureaucrat. Patient safety would be the clincher, senior management's Pavlovian bell. And having consulted his charts and data and complaints analyses, the medical director would come to the conclusion that Professor Nicholas Anderton, FRCS (Surgical Neurology), should be referred to the General Medical Council where his fitness to practise would be examined and his licence most likely suspended or revoked.

Anderton felt a mountainous rage against them all. His first thought was that he would defy them, not bow to their dictates or their scheming. He would carry on. Powerful people were rarely stopped by those around them; they made the rules, he would make the rules. He clung to the belief that, if he waited long enough, all the fuss and bother would die away, and he would be able to continue just as before. Yes, it would blow over and he would be just fine. And then he'd get even with the bastard Nash...

'Stop!' he admonished himself. This was paranoia, a lack of *aequanimitas*: that quality of serenity amid the storm, of imperturbability, the touchstone of the neurosurgeon since the days of Sir William Osler. There was no actual evidence, even circumstantial, of Nash's involvement in this latest humiliation. Anderton knew his feelings were tainted by envy and resentment towards a colleague who'd shone brighter than him and had climbed higher. He took a few deep breaths to calm himself.

The day after the operation on the Cushing's patient, Anderton had awoken with his heart pounding. He didn't remember being up in the night but neither did he feel refreshed – sleep apnoea, probably, a curse of fat people. The walls of the throat collapse; breathing stops, often for minutes at a time. He knew he would feel intensely drowsy during the day, would need more coffee than usual to get through the list. His jaws ached from grinding his teeth, and his hands felt clenched into balls even when he opened them flat. 'Hell,' he thought. 'This is no good.' He surveyed the rise of the sheet over his belly. A mountain to climb. He knew he should consider the operation.

When he'd composed himself again, he phoned his daughter Sophie. He always thought of her as 'needy Sophie'. But now he needed her, wanted to hear her voice.

He said, 'How are things, darling?'

'Well, you know... OK, really.'

'Uh-huh.'

'And you, Daddy. How are you doing?'

'Fine. Nothing to report.'

'That's good. Plenty of rare diseases and stuff, I hope.'

'More than enough, yes. You sure you're OK, darling? You sound little-voiced. Things not too hot?'

'Oh, *comme si comme ça*. Glimmers on the horizon, maybe. You know...'

'Good. Good. I'm thinking of going away for a few days. Having a break.'

'Good for you, Daddy.'

He wondered if he should discuss the operation with her. Though she was like her mother in having a mortal fear of fatness, at least in herself, she seemed to accept him for what he was. Even so, she'd probably encourage him to go ahead with the surgery. And no doubt Alyson would too, despite her fears and reservations; these days she even complained about his thighs rubbing together. But Anderton, who was not scared of fatness, had a mortal fear of doctors. Especially surgeons. He knew too much about them, how they thought. If one were to be cynical, this meant being unperturbed by leaving the patient dead, or fully aware but language-less, making abject noises, or in a persistent vegetative state. He knew: he'd done that to people, done it with *aequanimitas*.

It didn't help that in his mental hierarchy of merit, gastric surgeons occupied a place not far above wart-and-verruca nurses. Rabinovich was good, but even so. Although the operation was a simple one, there was so much that could go wrong, leaving aside the normal stuff like infection, haemorrhage, embolism or infarct. The tiny pouch of the new stomach could burst its seams, or you could get gallstones, the pain of which Anderton feared, because it was said to be worse than the pain of giving birth. Or the bloating, dizziness, diarrhoea and palpitations of 'dumping syndrome', where the new stomach propelled matter with unceremonious haste into the small intestine. Or the passage from the new stomach to the guts could become blocked and they'd have to perform further unpleasant procedures. Or thiamine deficiency leading to Korsakoff's syndrome – now wouldn't that be ironic. Or you could become intolerant of red meat, or shellfish, or other things that made life bearable. Not that the army of health advisors would allow you to eat enough of any of them to be worth the effort.

Anderton knew that if he agreed to the operation he'd lose agency, be delivered into the hands of not only surgeons, but a whole happy team of dieticians, psychologists, empathetic weight-loss surgery nurses, physiotherapists. And, God help him, support groups. On the other hand, when it came to his weight he hadn't had much agency to begin with. Not for many years. 'I can't help it,' he'd say to Alyson, and she'd raise one eyebrow. 'It's a matter of genes, something called fat mass and obesity-related transcript, and there's nothing I can do about it.' He knew that this was a half-truth at best. Genes predisposed you to fatness, they didn't force you to be fat.

And so his thoughts went round in circles. Some days he convinced himself he was happy in his skin, happy in his 128-kilo frame. That he need not conform to their expectations of thinness: Nash, Alyson, Bhattacharya and the rest of them. Damn them all! But, in the difficult moments when he struggled with his physical limitations – gasping for breath on the stairs, or unable properly to clean inaccessible parts of him, or fatigued after yet another bad night's sleep – he realised that he was telling himself a comforting lie.

Then, made anxious by too much introspection, he ate something, calmed down, carried on.

Alyson

Alyson pours herself a large glass of Scotch. Work is even more hellish than usual. One of her dodgy partners has failed to declare his suspicions regarding the property transactions of a member of the Russian mafia, allegedly. Nobody's telling her anything. Of course he didn't bloody declare them, he was in on it, it's obvious! But they're all being tarred with the same brush. The Solicitors Regulation Authority is investigating. Stressful times, more heavy drinking.

But she's coping.

She looks at herself in the mirror and says aloud, 'My name is Alyson and I am a high-functioning alcoholic. High-functioning, so that's OK, then.' She holds up her glass of Scotch. 'Cheers!' She drinks, and grins, and winks at herself.

Brain chemistry, she thinks, it's all to do with brain chemistry. What she knows is that hers has its own rhythms. She'll wake up with a head clear enough to work. On a good day, the ideas come by themselves, as if they've been lining up in an automated ideas factory while she was asleep: *I know – I'll use Part 3, Chapter 2, Section 18 of the Companies Act 2006*, that should sort the buggers... Then the mind's gradual seizing up throughout the morning, the zombified glaze of the early afternoon, the unquenchable need for a drink by the end of the day. Sometimes a lot earlier than that.

Before she knows it, she has lifted the glass again, and taken another gulp. Did she have free will just then? she wonders. Nobody forced her. True, there was the criminal act itself, the *actus reus*. But she didn't have awareness of the act, not in legal terms, didn't have the *mens rea*. How can you have free will when you do things without being aware of them? Aha, she's off the hook! Have another! Celebrate.

Then she thinks of Nick, eating compulsively. He can't help it, so he says, it's genetically determined. Recently she said to him, 'So you're giving up on free will? You have no control over your behaviours?'

He said, 'Free will is an illusion.'

'That's nonsense.'

'Thinking you chose to do something, and that your choice leads to an action, is just a trick of the brain. You kid yourself after the event, your brain revises truth and history as it goes along. They've done experiments to prove—'

'Trust you to find some fancy pseudo-scientific explanation for the fact you've got no willpower, Nick.'

He just smiled.

Sometimes he'll try to wind her up. He's like a bomb disposal expert wilfully setting off an explosion. He'll say things like, 'And do you have free will over your alcohol consumption, darling?'

She hates the way he can throw it back at her like that. It makes her lose it and scream at him. 'Look at you, you're fucking gross! How can you bear to be like that? And don't you even care about the fact you're killing yourself?'

Then it can become one of their bizarre Mexican standoffs:

> *I'll do something about my drinking if you*
> *do something about your eating.*
> *No, I'll do something about my eating when*
> *you do something about your drinking.*

How can they break the stalemate?

She thinks of the dodgy partner in her law firm and wonders if he'll be able to argue that he committed his money-laundering act without meaning to, that he didn't do it *knowingly* or *purposefully*. Come on, the law's not that much of an ass. And therefore, she thinks, I'm guilty, guilty as hell, guilty of drinking while in control of my own free will. Fuck, she hates these internal debates. She finds herself reaching for the glass.

Nick says the skull is like a bone box, with the brain trapped inside. When the pressure builds up within the skull, the only way for the brain to escape is for it to squeeze out through the small hole at the bottom, like cake icing. Not good. Best thing for a brain to do is to stay put, reduce the pressure. Is her marriage like that? Best to stay put, reduce the pressure? *Per potum*, perhaps. The question makes her feel she's going to explode.

The Turkish saddle

Anderton knew the difference between good and bad, nourishing and unhealthy foods, but it was all the same to him. He was not a lyric gourmand but an epic one. He could consume a gastronomic burger of buffalo or wild boar from a hip eatery round the corner from the hospital, only to top it up within the hour with a KFC Mighty Bucket, followed by a full bar of milk chocolate. He ate with relish, sometimes with cramming urgency, occasionally with delicacy, taking slow, contemplative mouthfuls. People – Gianluca, for example – sometimes wondered how a man who loved fine Italian or Spanish food could also stuff himself with junk. Anderton supposed that it was a bit like the fellow who was married to a beautiful, sophisticated wife but still felt the need to go kerb-crawling. Such things were beyond explanation, but they happened.

Whenever he stopped eating there was misery and the emptiness. He hadn't always been like this. At least, the condition had never been so full-blown,

so *florid*. It was since the catastrophes – first professional, then personal.

Neurosurgeons were supposed to put their mistakes behind them, learn the general lesson and
forget the particular disaster by the time of the next
ward round or the next operation. But the memory
of this one disaster consumed him. He'd gnaw
away at it, recalling the day, early summer 2007,
in minute detail, analysing every move, re-dissect-
ing every decision. He'd been the author of his own
misery with his arrogance, his ego, his acting like
a capricious deity determining the fate of mortals.
He recalled Alyson saying, soon after he became a
consultant, that he had a bully's instincts: always
looking for weaknesses in colleagues, especially
underlings. She'd fed back to him reports of junior
doctors in tears after one of his tickings-off. 'You
need to harden your shell if you are going to survive
as a neurosurgeon,' he'd say to moping colleagues.
He became a moping colleague himself.

In the immediate wake of the incident, he
worried about the pending case conference at which
Nash would expose his responsibility for the failure.
And the inevitable interview with the hospital's
director of governance, and the letter of complaint
from the family's solicitor, the consequent appear-
ance before a panel of august individuals who would
pass judgement on him. He'd lie awake, staring at
the ceiling, his mind churning through the details
to no purpose. Some nights, Alyson would stir

long enough to murmur, 'You stink of bone dust. Didn't you even shower?' He had hoped her lawyer's skills would help him steer a clear line through the tangled heaps of evidence, motive, reasoning. But she had her own troubles, and she grew impatient with his self-pity and his sense of doom.

He feared he'd been shorn of the aura of authority that consultant neurosurgeons gave off. His colleagues looked at him differently – some with malice, some contempt. Some – this was the worst – with sympathy: the consoling pat on the arm, the murmured condolence, 'Sorry to hear about...' or, 'There but for the...' Before all this, they'd never have dared. He grieved for the eminence he'd been. People said you became a better surgeon because of your errors: they became part of you, made you who you were, gave you a broader perspective, greater empathy. But his error was a massive tumour, invading his sense of self. He couldn't excise it.

Weeks turned into months, into years.

His overeating, always an occasional flourish in his life of big appetites, became chronic. Within a few months, his weight had ballooned. It was as if he'd reverted to the pattern laid down in childhood, the podgy schoolboy reborn. At home he found no solace or relief. Alyson shrank from him. If she spoke, it was to scold his self-absorption, his constant eating; just the soft clunk of the fridge door closing could provoke her. Or she treated him to her cutting sarcasm, raising the stakes. He thought of moving to a less glamorous, less demanding post, somewhere outside London, in the 'provinces'.

*

His self-flagellation often started with the same visual memory: of his fellow consultant, Alasdair Nash, showing off to the trainees. Nash and half a dozen young medics crammed into a window-less room. The most junior doctor bringing up the scans on the computer screen. Nash shining his laser pen at the image of a brain, dark with small close-scattered white patches. Saying, 'This looks like a playroom after a toddler's birthday party. Hard to say whose handiwork, certain-ly not mine.' Nash clicking his fingers, the next slide. 'Compare and contrast. Here's one I did earlier.' A nervous stutter of laughter rippling round the room. Nash swaggering. 'Complete resection of the meningioma. Massive though it was. All gone. No mess, no loose ends, took the trouble to clear up after myself. Good probability of non-recurrence. Questions?'

Anderton's senior surgical trainee in those days, breathless Rachel Eaves, or his ambitious registrar, Jamie Boxall, were always telling him how fast Nash worked in theatre, how complete his debulk-ing of tumours, how clean his clipping of the tricky necks of aneurysms, how nifty his fingerwork in the posterior intracranial fossa close to the brain stem.

Clearly, Boxall aspired to be like Nash. To *be* Nash. Not to be Anderton. The registrar even started adopting Nash's speech mannerisms, his born-to-rule diction.

What had the man done to deserve all this ad-ulation? He was a competent surgeon, true, but no more so than Anderton, and polished his reputation by avoiding the really difficult cases. He was clever at self-promotion and cultivating the right people, knew how to pull strings on key committees; took credit for triumphs, deflected blame, usually onto juniors. He published inexplicably influential papers in *Neurosurgery*. 'Don't bother with the sedation,' Anderton would say to Bhattacharya, 'just give the patient Nash's latest piece.' Oh, and there was his private work, operating lucratively on hopeless grade 4 glioblastomas in the brains of UAE prince-lings. Bastard!

'You're obsessed with him,' Alyson said, after one such rant.

'I am not! He's a run-of-the-mill surgeon and a genius at self-promotion. Why are you defending him?'

'I'm not. You're obsessed.'

Nash had once been Anderton's friend, in a jostling, competitive way. At medical school, they'd revise for the clinical examinations to-gether. They'd tried to outdo one another or trip each other up, flinging out obscure symptoms for diseases of the liver, or misleading signs of lung emboli, or esoteric abnormalities of gait. In their spare time, they drank together, slept with women from the same circle, fell out, made up over a pint or two. Nash persuaded Anderton to join the rugby club, because you mixed with blokes who were going places, who attracted a better class of female.

Anderton was flattered by this friendship in spite, or because of, the fact that his North London accent, by now a déclassé, metropolitan drawl, did not have the public-school polish and assurance of Nash's. But there was always a jousting edge to it, even as students.

'You going out with that skinny girl?' Nash said on one occasion.

'Why? You interested?' Anderton smiled, pleased to have noticed something too eager about the way Nash said the word 'skinny'.

'Not a medic, is she?' Nash continued. 'Fucking law student or something.'

'Alyson.'

'Yeah.'

'And…?'

'She fits the pattern.'

'The pattern?' Anderton regretted rising to the bait. Nash would sense a chink in his defences.

'Same as all your others. Thin and pale. Like those cadavers we had to dissect in year two. And like them they all move v-e-r-y slowly. The undead.'

'Fuck off.'

'Perhaps you have necrophiliac tendencies, Anderton.' He added, '*Ah, he loves the smell of putre-faction in the morning!* Or maybe it's the formalin…'

'Fantasies, fantasies. I'm sure the morgue technician can help you out.' Anderton flipped his beer mat off the table, caught it, flipped it again, dropped it.

'...though, of course, if they're undead,' Nash went on, 'then technically speaking it would be *a*necrophiliac.'

After finals, and two years as house officers, they followed the same route into neurosurgery. Their paths then separated as they worked through their training in different hospitals, and rose from junior trainee to registrar to senior clinician. Anderton excelled in theoretical knowledge and surgical practice; he had good hands. Nash was a pin-sharp clinician, a good observer, skilled at displaying empathy with nervous patients, unfurling his white smile. When Anderton, still a registrar, heard that Nash had been appointed consultant at a London teaching hospital, he felt a gut lurch of envy. He knew he ought to ring to congratulate him, get it out the way. But when Nash answered the call, Anderton blurted, 'Bloody hell, how d'you wangle that, you jammy bugger?' He'd meant it to sound humorous, but it came out wrong, peeved. Nash replied, with killing condescension, 'Yeah, a lucky break. But you're perfectly capable, Anderton, your time will come.'

And in time, Anderton did get his consultant's post, in the same London hospital. It was the place you aimed for if you had talent and ambition. At first, he was dazzled by the simple change that took place when you entered theatre, not as registrar but as consultant. Swathed in the sterile robes, he was the high priest at the altar, no longer an acolyte. The patient would make the due blood sacrifice and, if lucky, survive. Everything was the same, and everything had changed.

He was so blinded by the sense of having 'arrived' that it took him a while to notice that he and Nash were no longer friends, not even friendly rivals; simply rivals. In difficult cases, Anderton found himself asking against his own instincts, What would Nash do? He wanted to retain *aequanimitas*. But, to an unconfessable degree, his colleague got under his skin: a small voice within saying, *Nash* would take the whole thing out, *Nash* would resect the affected dura *and* the bone, *Nash* would work for ten hours if necessary, twenty even, to tease the tumour capsule away from all those vital structures. Probably piss in his scrubs rather than waste time on comfort breaks. Nash's battle cries of *total resection!* and *no tumour left behind!* echoed in Anderton's mind until he wanted to scream.

A patient named Paul Hayden came for an appointment in Anderton's clinic. In his thirties, affable, a software engineer, a marathon runner. He'd been having blurred vision in one eye for months, then in both, 'a loss of visual acuity' as the notes had it. Also, headaches which were worsening. The scans showed a large meningioma, a tumour of the membranes surrounding the brain. It grew up and out from behind the sella turcica, a dip in the winged bone at the base of the skull. The growth was not cancerous but had started to push back and invade surrounding tissue. Untreated, it would damage the brain, make Hayden blind, and probably kill him.

'The dilemma for the surgeon,' Anderton explained, 'and hence for the patient, is that the more you remove, the higher the risks. On the other hand, we could leave a safe amount behind, but the less you remove, the greater the chance of it coming back and being a problem in the future.'

'I see.' Paul Hayden sat with his chin in his hand. He swallowed and looked at Anderton. 'So, you're the expert. What's your advice?'

The meningioma was extensive and complicated. It would be pressing on the optic nerves, millimetres from the internal carotid arteries and the stalk of the pituitary gland, possibly already engulfing them. It would be a challenge. So much to go wrong. Great benefits for Paul Hayden if it came off and, of course, kudos for Anderton. Alisdair Nash hadn't wanted to take this case on: a warning sign perhaps. But if he *had*, he would have gone for total resection, the full works.

'If it were me,' Anderton said at last, 'I'd want to get it all out.'

'OK. Good,' said Hayden. 'Let's go for it. Fortune favours the brave, as they say.'

Aware that this was almost certainly untrue most of the time, at least in neurosurgery, Anderton gave a small tight smile. 'Fortune favours the *brain*,' he said.

Hayden nodded in his energetic, friendly way. 'Amen to that, and toes and fingers crossed, eh.'

*

Bhattacharya scanned his monitors. 'All well. As Napoleon remarked, "I don't need a good general, I need a lucky one."'

'You're implying I'm not a good surgeon, Pranab, just a lucky one?' muttered Anderton without taking his eyes away from the operating microscope.

'The question, as always, is how to be both, Prof, how to be both.'

Anderton smiled. 'Anaesthetists just have to be good.'

'You're saying I'm unlucky?'

'You're a fucking albatross.'

'Thank you.'

Anderton looked up fondly at the tall anaesthetist and added, 'Twelve-foot wingspan and all that.'

Earlier, as always, he had selected the music with care. 'Something *energetic* I fancy this morning,' he'd said to Boxall. 'But not *too* energetic. Not Wagner, more Mozart. Upbeat. Some jolly horn for the gross debulking, followed by the clarinet concerto for the tricky part. Bhattacharya quite likes a bit of Mozart. Not that anaesthetists have to do the tricky part, but still, we'll humour him.' It was possible that Boxall did not like a bit of Mozart, but this was neither here nor there. His time would come, busy bustling little Boxall, with his floppy dark hair and calculating eyes, whose ambition knew no bounds.

'Consider it done,' Boxall said, in a tone that sounded to Anderton both fawning and sly.

Hours later, with the cheerfully chivvying strains of the closing rondo of Mozart's Clarinet Concerto in his ears for the second time (or was it the third?), Anderton turned to his registrar. 'I think I'm done here, Boxall, I'll leave you to close up and dispose of the junk.'

The operation had gone remarkably well. He'd coagulated the base of the tumour to stop its blood supply, sucked its guts out using the aspirator, detached it with meticulous decisiveness from the surrounding brain, the optic nerve and the carotid artery. He'd extracted all visible tumour, along with the parts of the dura and bone where it had encroached. So many things might have gone wrong but hadn't.

At some point, hours in, he knew he should stop, leave a little behind. The remaining portion was tricky, pushing up against the fiddly white cords of nerves and vascular branches that ran through the narrow cranial spaces. He'd hesitated, trying not to let doubts form. Yet he couldn't help worrying that

Nash hadn't taken the case. Was it because he'd not wanted to risk his performance indicators, sully his treasured collection of before-and-after scans? Or perhaps he'd booked in for an early-evening round of golf with the clinical director? As he mused about Nash, Anderton became aware of Boxall's eyes on him, of Bhattacharya's concerned frown. And, as if his fingers were taking charge of his brain, he began again, prodding, snipping, sucking away. Now he'd have to hold that steady nerve. He felt like an acrobat balancing on one hand on top of a tall building: a second's lapse in concentration from catastrophe.

A spurt of blood obscuring his view, some small vessel cut through – catastrophe beckoning. Anxious minutes searching for the source of the leak. A battle between blood flow and the suction tip. A sense of blundering into the fearsomely fragile stuff of mind. He'd seen it before, as a young house officer: the nicked artery, the bloodstorm; the young man left a howling husk, unable to return from the far-off shore where language made no sense.

But, at last, the swirl of blood cleared. Anderton could make out the terrain once more. He plugged the leak, clamping, cauterising. His breathing softened, his equilibrium returned.

Finally, the tumour capsule was peeled away, extracted, and the battle won. Anderton relaxed, humming to himself. The main thing in his mind was that the 'after' MRI would show a triumphantly complete removal of the tumour. He'd tell the patient,

Hayden, about the low risk of recurrence, tell him to go and live a normal life. His trainees would have something to aspire to: the gold standard. Nash would have something to think about.

Anderton went home, wearily exultant.

Early the following morning, the phone rang, waking him from deep sleep. It was the doctor on duty in the neurosurgical intensive care unit. The pressure in Hayden's skull was high and rising. They'd given him medication to bring it down, to no effect. His blood pressure was also up. Christ! thought Anderton. It could be a stroke, death of brain tissue, severe swelling, triggered very possibly by some intricate manoeuvre in the final high-risk stages of the operation, or by a new bleed from the minor artery he'd damaged. Or something else, something else. *Why had he not stopped in time? Why had he insisted on getting every last speck of tumour out?* The duty doctor said they were investigating the problem. 'I want him scanned,' said Anderton, his voice irritable and thick with sleep. 'I want him scanned by the time I get there.'

He drove fast to the hospital. If the pressure was still rising, an emergency craniotomy would be on the cards. But then the brain might swell out of the hole in the skull, and that genie could never be got back in its bottle. He cursed his over-ambition, his gung-ho approach. He remembered Bhattacharya's words on some other mournful occasion, uttered in his lugubrious, humorous tones: 'As the saying goes, Nick, "Another victory like that and we're done for".'

Anderton arrived on the ward to find the patient surrounded by medical staff. The duty doctor looked up. 'Both pupils blown.'

'Well, that's that, then,' said Anderton, 'we're too bloody late. Bloody hell! He'll have coned, for Christ's sake.' The pressure had built up in Hayden's head until it squeezed parts of the brain out through the foramen magnum, the 'great hole' at the base of the skull through which the spinal cord passes. The extruded matter would crush the brain stem, terminating awareness, stilling breath. The endgame.

The duty doctor remained miserably mute. The man that had been Paul Hayden was still alive, but not meaningfully so. He was lying on his back, legs stiffly straight, toes stretching towards the far mattress, his head and neck arched backwards. He looked like a follower of some strange cult, invoking his harsh deity.

'Somebody better contact the family,' Anderton said. His colleagues looked at him. He shook his head, resigned. 'I'll do it.'

*

Once all the inquiries and investigations were done, the lessons learned, the pompous moralising and patronising advice delivered, Anderton slowly mended. He started to operate again with some of his old assurance, and for a time the sheer presence of his growing bulk seemed to renew his surgical authority, though he now took a conservative approach to difficult meningiomas. Sometimes one of his patients would die. Usually there was nothing that he could have done differently. He would tell himself, as he told his students, that neurosurgery could only advance by error, by constant probing of the frontiers of what was possible; that belief, even hubris, was necessary for progress. That often in neurosurgery you were simply unlucky, that stuff happened. And so he tried to convince himself of something that was unconvincing, until flashbacks of the Hayden case came to knock him off balance. He'd hear again Nash's voice at the Morbidity and Mortality Conference following Paul Hayden's death: 'Who in their right mind would attempt a total resection of a big meningioma, in that location? The clinical picture called for partial resection only' – a glance round the room – 'precisely to avoid this outcome.'

And, though it was a painful process, Anderton began to acknowledge that it wasn't the grossness or the boldness of his error that bothered him – he'd cocked up fatally before and no doubt would again. No, it was the false belief that had led to it: that what mattered most to him was to out-compete Nash, to put one over on him. His rival had got inside his head. Nash had won. Anderton would falter at such moments, his self-belief would dissolve, he'd see again the instrument in his hand, the sudden cloud of blood. He tried to banish the images from his mind.

He'd go to the fridge, or the secret stash in his desk drawer. Eat, forget. Remember. Eat.

Alyson

Alyson learns that there are things called mirror neurons. Nick has told her so. She is apparently supposed to find this interesting.

'What the fuck are mirror neurons?'

It seems that when you're watching someone performing an action, these neurons fire in the same parts of the brain as when you're doing the action yourself.

'OK. And why do we care...?'

Because, Nick says, it's about the way you learn through imitation. For example, Sophie watching other ice skaters do a move and then copying them.

She thinks, Is that how you learned to be such an arrogant prick, Anderton, by imitating the likes of Alisdair Nash?

And also, he explains, it's about how you acquire empathy and knowledge of the *minds* of others. Which is very ironic, Alyson thinks, as her husband is one of the least empathetic people she knows. At least, when it comes to her. No doubt in the past he's been very empathetic with that scrub nurse,

Janette, or whatever her grubby little pole-dancer name is. He may know a lot about brains but has very little understanding of the minds of others. His own mind is obsessively focused on his work. Or on food. Or on pole dancers, or whatever. Even on the kids sometimes. Just not on her.

She remembers the trouble at work. He was moping around for weeks, months. Oh the strain, oh the stress, oh the awful bloody catastrophe! Going over and over it until she was sick of listening to him. These days, it's his snoring and wheezing that keep her awake. She can hear him through the wall – he makes the whole house vibrate, like a washing machine on a slow spin cycle. Sometimes she'll go into his bedroom late at night, sneak a look at him. She is appalled and fascinated by the way his breathing seems to stop, the way he gulps for breath in his sleep.

She did feel sorry for him in some ways, after his medical disaster. She wasn't happy that Nash managed to get one over on him. She doesn't like to see a grown man humiliated, not even her husband. No one can rile Anderton like Nash can, even now, after all these years. Not even Sophie. In fact, Anderton and Sophie rub along well enough. Their prickles and spines must face opposite ways.

Alyson has known Alisdair Nash since student days, when they were in the same crowd of snooty rugger-bugger groupies. She was quite interested in him for a time, even though he was a cocky bastard.

Or because of that. One drunken night she found herself dancing slowly with him at some party. He was all over her, like the octopus in that Japanese erotic print, but in a bad way. Up close there's something repulsive about him, oleaginous and slimy. His tongue in her ear and rubbing his hard-on up against her thigh – no shame. She managed to pull his tentacles off her and get back to her girlfriends. They had a good laugh about it.

These days he still grins salaciously at her, like there was once something between them. Which, in a manner of speaking, there was.

Not long after the octopus episode, she'd got together with Anderton. Partly because they both loved the same music: Mozart concertos, Bach, Purcell. Ali Farka Touré, raunchy hip-grinding lover's rock, the Gypsy Kings. They hit it off being scathing together about other people's musical tastes. He also pretended to like books. She knew it was a ploy to get her into bed, though she couldn't care less if he read or not. In fact, he'd only read two books in his life, other than medical textbooks, and then only because some ex-girlfriend had nagged him to: *The Old Man and the Sea*, which he quite enjoyed as he was rooting for the old guy; and *The Metamorphosis*, which he said was boring and not plausible. But still, at least he had read them. What would he think about *The Metamorphosis* these days, she wonders, having turned from a man into a great pink slug?

The relationship was very intense in the early years. She was turned on by his confidence, his appetites, his single-minded ambition to make himself into a neurosurgeon. By the fact he was the son of a butcher; he knew flesh. He was exotic to her, glamorous, a high-flyer, going places. It was all very volatile but exciting. They stuck together, and they found, despite themselves, that they couldn't be unstuck. Even after he fucked other women, and things went sour. *Bastard*. Not that she was blameless, but he drove her to it.

Penfield's homunculus

Anderton would go over it all in his mind as if making a witness statement: *I came back from work earlier than expected that day, my last operation having been cancelled. On arriving at my home in Horsley Avenue, I found my wife, Alyson Seymour (she insisted on retaining her maiden name), in bed with another man.*

He was still reeling from the surgical disaster of a few weeks earlier. And now this second traumatic event, almost predictable since sorrows did not come as single spies, as Alyson was always telling him.

*

Alyson. In *their* bed. With another man. His wife in bed with another man. Screwing. Noisily. The fact of it was not just traumatic but almost unthinkable.

They'd met, all those years ago, in the students' union bar, its carpet sticky underfoot. He experienced a fleeting but vivid olfactory memory of stale beer and vomit. There was something about the way she stood – skinny, languid, loose-limbed, flexible, conscious of her appeal. Her eyes suggested a readiness for sexual mischief. In bed, it was as if she'd thrown off her prim middle-class upbringing and plunged into a world of sensual experimentation, determined to try it all, pulling Anderton in after her. The salacious chat with the rugby club crowd at the students' union seemed painfully callow and laddish; this was the real thing. He was smitten: he liked her wriggling body and uninhibited cries during sex and – when they managed to drag themselves from the bed – her abrasive humour and sharp observations, her ability to hold her drink, sparkle in groups, draw envious glances. Was impressed by her knowledge of literature, and her ambition to be a lawyer who would make things happen.

At first, Alyson had pretensions to educate him, rub off the rough edges. But she gave up when she realised he wasn't going to share her tastes, was too practical a man to read fiction, particularly the literary kind that required intellectual effort. He announced that he'd stick to medical textbooks and the occasional thriller. 'What, no girly mags?' asked Alyson tartly. He admired her intellectual hinterland but had little desire to share it. He preferred her debauched and abandoned.

They had moved in together. He was deep into his surgical training, she getting articles in a busy London practice and already dreaming of partnership. Lust faded. He flirted with other women, because he could, because he couldn't help it, because it made him feel alive. He and Alyson argued, pondered a split. One day around this time, she called him at work.

'I'm fucking pregnant, Anderton.'

'Can't you get...?'

'No I bloody can't.'

Once he'd held his daughter, whom they named Sophie, felt her squirm in his tentative arms, heard her heart-stopping mewls, he would always deny even to himself that he'd ever said or thought that his wife should not have the baby. Alyson took maternity leave, lost traction in the law firm, fell pregnant again. She resented the children, but mainly she resented him. He'd fondly call them 'our two little clinical misjudgements'. For her they were forces of chaos, disrupting her attempts to establish some fragile order in her world. 'I'm sick of being a fucking baby machine to help propagate Anderton genes!' she'd scream. He'd shrug and go to work.

She became a haggard mother run ragged by small children. She no longer made an effort for him, and if she did, he wasn't enticed. And yet he found it strange to discover that he could not leave her now that they had kids. It was neither duty nor honour, it was simply that Sophie and Ben had changed something in him just by existing. He felt bound to them by blood, paternal love, something disquietingly selfless and painful. And though part of him wanted to get out, to start afresh, another part needed Alyson. He'd grown dependent on her and their scratchy marriage.

He'd get back from work, exhausted, shut himself in his study and turn on his computer. The kids would be stomping round the house and he'd hear Alyson shouting at them. He needed twenty minutes to clear his head of work before facing them all. He'd sit and stare at the screen, playing idly with the bronze Penfield homunculus that he used as a paperweight on his desk and which was inscribed 'To Professor Nicholas Anderton, with gratitude, from the Neurosurgical Department of the Sir Hitesh Saroha Hospital, Delhi.' The homunculus showed how different parts of the body mapped onto the brain's cerebral cortex. When you made a model representing body parts according to the size of their corresponding brain regions, it turned out to be a horrid, large-headed little fellow, with massive hands, lips and tongue, and intimidating genitalia. For Anderton, it was a cross between an executive toy and a talisman, easing the stress from him.

Alyson would burst in and yell at him for not helping with the kids. He'd stare at her. He didn't want to lose his temper, because keeping it put him in the right and infuriated her more. He often used his damned reasonableness as a weapon.

'I need a few moments' quiet time. You can't switch modes from one minute to the next.'

'Quiet time! I'd *love* some quiet time. You work twelve hours every day, and when you're not at work you're thinking about it. Or staring at that bloody screen. Or chasing after that scrubber nurse.'

'*Scrub* nurse. And I'm not chasing after her.' This half-lie was out before he could stop it: it was Jenna who'd been chasing after him in her cheery, guilt-free way.

Alyson blew out an exasperated breath. 'What about me, Anderton? Where do I fit in your over-stuffed schedule?'

Riled by his refusal to shout back, to escalate the argument, she gave one of her malign smiles and said, 'And apparently you do lose your cool at work, and throw things. Rumour has it.'

'Where did you get that from?'

'Chucking scalpels around the operating theatre, so I hear.'

'I've never thrown a scalpel in my life. Health and safety and all that.' Strictly speaking true – the instrument in question was not a scalpel but a pituitary rongeur. 'Don't believe everything people tell you. Now, would you like me to read to Sophie, or bathe Ben?'

'Yes. Both.'

*

That afternoon, the afternoon it happened, Anderton had let himself in and put down his bag on the parquet floor of the hall. He was on his way to the kitchen when he heard the high-pitched yelping. It came from above him, somewhere in the house. He recognised the sound, though he'd never heard it from a distance. Its familiarity was unsettling. He slipped off his black tasselled moccasins, crept up the stairs, listened for a moment to the noises from the bedroom. He flung open the door, startling the pair of them into frozen postures of fear and embarrassment.

The man, who was turned away from the door, sat up.

It was Jamie Boxall, Anderton's registrar.

'For fuck's sake,' said Alyson, 'I wasn't expecting you back, what are you doing back?' Absurdly, she covered her breasts with the sheet.

Anderton ignored her. He was staring at Boxall, who started to say, 'Well, this is awkward, erm…' Anderton cut him short. 'Get out! Get out of my bloody house! Out! Out! Now!'

Boxall lifted his legs over the side of the bed, covering his crotch with both hands, and bent down to retrieve his underpants. Anderton was aware of the name 'SAXX' emblazoned on the waistband of the boxer briefs as Boxall shuffled them up his thighs and over his pale rump, and of flitting images of his family sitting down to eat their evening meal when he was a child, a large drum of Saxa salt on the table and his father signalling for it with his long fingers.

As the wife-shagger hunched over to pull on his jeans, Anderton said, 'And you better find yourself a new bloody job in a new bloody hospital.'

Leaving Alyson sobbing on the bed, he went downstairs and out to the garage so as not to see Boxall again. He prowled the confined space, listening for the soft click of the front door closing. When he heard it, he let himself cry with rage. He pounded his fist into the exposed brickwork until his knuckles bled, shouting, 'Fuck Alyson! Fuck her, fuck her!' In a while he'd composed himself enough to get in the car and drive to the shops at the top of the High Street. He went into McDonald's and ordered a double cheeseburger, French fries and a large Coke. In the upstairs dining area, he found an empty table and sat with his back to the window. As he ate, he felt the agitation drain from his system and equanimity return.

*

Alyson stood in his study and said, 'I think I love him.'

He felt a chill ripple down from the top of his head to the base of his spine. His lips worked, but he couldn't speak. Her rages, the bitter arguments, were better than this. Anger, OK. But not love. Why bring love into it?

'Haven't you got anything to say?'

Anderton said, 'In love? With that homunculus?'

'What? What are you talking about? I may leave you, Nick.'

'And the kids?'

'Jamie and I have talked about it, he'd be happy to—'

Anderton tried to contain himself, remain cool and cutting, but he couldn't. 'You've talked about it, for God's sake? You can't be serious. Bloody hell! I won't allow that freak near my children.'

'It's not your choice.'

'It *is* my bloody choice…'

'And you can get off your moral high horse. As if you were the injured party.'

'Oh, what? *You're* the injured party?'

'You've never shown me any consideration, or paid any attention to me. Is it any wonder—'

'That's not true.'

'And you've let yourself go. You've been piling it on.'

'That's a bit of an exaggeration. It's only been—'

'What? Since that trouble at work? Come off it. You're always eating. You have a full meal and then in half an hour you're stuffing yourself again. Junk half the time. Pure greed, no self-control.'

'I've put on a bit, but I'm middle-aged, for Christ's sake! People do. Why would—'

'It's not as if…' She stopped and shook her head, too furious to speak.

'As if what?'

'Jamie told me about you and the scrub nurse. That it *was* true.'

'Well, Boxall would say that, wouldn't he. There's nothing to it. At all.'

Only a quick blow job after the Christmas party, a bit of flirting. He'd put a stop to it immediately, of course – *that was a bit of a mistake, Jenna.* She'd laughed mischievously and put her fingers to her lips. *Oops! I like little mistakes. And you didn't seem too bothered at the time!* He'd felt quite anxious for a day or two. He'd said, 'Look, we have to work together.' Jenna had smiled, not pushing the game too far. *Fair enough. Not a problem.* And it hadn't been.

'And the Christmas present?' said Alyson, arms crossed, head nodding as if in self-validation.

'What?' Anderton for a moment was genuinely stumped. 'What are you talking about?'

'Holy Father! Give me a fucking drink. You know what I'm talking about.'

'Do I?'

'That whiny little junior – Laura, was it? – and her so-called "Christmas present".'

Oh shit, Anderton thought. That. That was donkey's years ago. Just before Christmas, when the kids were still young. There'd been a phone call, no one on the line when he answered. Then, a knock at the door. It was Lauren, the neurosurgical trainee. He was still a registrar in those days. She looked so young, but at the same time her face was pinched and sour. 'Hello,' she'd said, once she could see Anderton's wife standing in the hallway behind him, near the mistletoe. 'Thought you'd like an early Christmas present.' She patted the bulge of her belly. 'It's yours, I'm pretty sure. If it's a boy, I'm going to call him Thomas. Well, say hello. Say, "Hello Thomas!" Tommy, I'll call him.' Anderton had stood there, open-mouthed but speechless. He was still trying to stutter some response when she looked up and smiled, and said, 'Anyway, Happy Christmas!' With that, she was gone. But why would it have had anything to do with him? Perhaps it hadn't, perhaps she was going round all the men she'd slept with. She'd not said anything before about being pregnant. They'd had a fling, yes, but only a brief one; these things were going to happen when you spent so many hours cooped up at work with the same people, very intense. Life and death going on. And she'd told him she was on the pill, damn it. And anyway, he'd put an end to it as soon as he realised she was getting serious. Too late, obviously.

Alyson, well, the kids needed her, she carried on. They carried on.

Years earlier, when he was still a very junior doctor, there'd been this patient of his, Ms K, Madeleine Kendall. He'd never told Alyson about her, and she'd never found out. In one sense, there'd been nothing to tell, and at the same time, everything. Working a run of nights in a row, he'd fallen for her, badly. Madeleine – Maddy – was hauntingly pale and wasting away; they couldn't fix her. His feelings for her shocked him, something powerful had knocked him flying. He hadn't known such unsettling emotions before, hadn't realised there were things beyond lust and mutual need and occasional affection. He'd sit at Maddy's bedside chatting to her, making excuses not to go home to a fretful wife and two infants. Their exchanges had an unnerving intimacy. She was his own age, pretty; but there was also her gaze, there were the looks that passed between them, the chemistry, electricity. And for once, electricity and chemistry felt like more than metaphors, because that was how the brain worked: electrical signals, chemical reactions were what made it tick. They instilled the elusive deeper meanings of the few banal words Anderton and Maddy managed to exchange. Once, he took her hand and held it in silence for a long time. She looked up at him and smiled. He felt dismayed, his equilibrium disturbed, because he could not rationalise this, could not map these strange sensations to the usual hedonic hotspots, the pleasure centres and circuits of the brain. They were painful pleasures, quite unlike anything he'd known. Unlike the joys of screwing, say, or eating. They were *love*, a word he turned over in his mind like some shiny alien element. They made him deeply unhappy and afraid.

'You may have forgotten, but I haven't,' Alyson was saying.

'So what do you want to do?'

'Do?' she said crossly. 'What do you mean, "do"?'

'You're old enough to be his... aunt, for Christ's sake.'

'He loves me.'

Anderton chuckled. 'Of course he does. Auntie Alyson. Poor lamb.'

'Fuck you. Have you looked in the mirror lately? At least I haven't let myself go.'

'Well, at least I haven't screwed anybody other than you on our marital bed.' This wasn't strictly true. But it had only been that once, with Lauren, when Alyson had taken the kids to visit their grandmother in Scotland.

He picked Penfield's homunculus off the desk and started toying with it, stroking the outsized lips and extremities. 'And the kids, is he prepared to take them on? And what about in five years' time, when you're older and more unappetising, is he still going to want you?'

'I'm going out,' she said, 'the air's unbreathable round here.'

'"*Love him*"? Spare me.'

She moved towards the door.

'Hang on.' He held out the homunculus to her. 'Why don't you give him this? Tell him I thought there was quite a likeness.'

In the following weeks a weary stalemate developed between them. Both were busy with work, and when they spoke about practical things they managed a business-like civility. Perhaps sensing the parental strains, the kids – now adolescent – were demanding. Anderton would attend to one, usually Sophie, helping with her homework, or her fallouts with friends, or her teenage existential angst, while Alyson devoted herself to the other, usually Ben. Boxall, meanwhile, had gone to earth, contriving to get himself seconded to a rotation in Hertford for six weeks, a specialist placement in stereotaxy. When Anderton made allusions to his absence, Alyson was evasive.

Eventually, Anderton learned on the grapevine that Boxall had moved to Canada to take up a post in a hospital in Nova Scotia. Alyson brooded for some months, sinking into lethargy, before slowly emerging into her usual acid tetchiness. She made clear the marriage did not satisfy her, that staying was second best. She began to drink more heavily. Anderton didn't try to stop her because it made her more liveable-with, less spiky, at least for a while. Slowly things returned to a kind of soured normality.

*

Neurosurgery was not an introspective vocation, on the whole. You were too busy doing the tricky, tiring day-to-day work to engage in philosophical considerations about mind and matter. And yet, entering the path lab one day and watching the pathologist remove the brain from the skull of a patient and balance it on his hand, Anderton had the impulse to take it from him, feel it, weigh it, get the sense of it. Standing in this place of the dead, he was hit suddenly, yet again, with the thought that this wobbling lump of smooth-textured pâté was where mind resided. That this brain was, or once had been, mindful, full of mind; had held cognition, emotion, memory somewhere, though nowhere in particular. Had contained a life lived. And this was all there was, a greying paste, in which neurons had once fired and mysterious chemistry had fizzed at the synapses.

Leaving the lab, Anderton felt pangs of hunger. He imagined entering Le Frattaglie and sitting at one of its square wooden tables with their red and white chequered tablecloths. He would greet Gianluca and tuck into a good *fegato alla veneziana*, comfortingly aromatic, with caramelised onions and red wine; or perhaps a *frittura di cervelli e zucchine*. Or both. They would sit together after the meal over a digestif – Cynar perhaps, with its dark, bitter-sweet flavour – and be two fat middle-aged men, knowledgeable about the finer points of butchery, talking of cuts of beef and pork.

For a moment or two he fought a half-hearted battle against temptation, then gave in. His appetite meant he was still alive.

Alyson

Alyson smiles to herself, a little grimly. If she's honest, the homunculus does look a bit like Boxall – he does have quite big hands, big lips, and the rest. Therefore she hates Anderton for having pointed it out. The thought cannot be unthought, damn him. Actually, Nick himself is rather like the homunculus: driven by his desires, and his base rivalries, and his lust for kudos and scrubber nurses. If she made a homunculus of him, she'd have the belly enormous, and the forehead would be a great convex dome bulging out under the pressure of the mighty brain. At one time, he'd have had an outsized dick, but not these days – more of a mi-cro-dick. He once explained to her how they got the Penfield model by sticking pins in the brains of awake patients and seeing where in the body they felt the sensation. Like vivisection, she thinks. Anderton would never understand why she gets so het up about the idea of sticking pins in your brain: into the thing you feel, remember, plan, analyse with. She has electric prickles of discomfort down her belly and groin just thinking about it. The idea is too gruesome; only a man would come up with it.

And anyway, why a homunculus, why not a femuncula? Didn't they do the experiments on women too? She learned Latin at school, so she knows homunculus means 'little man' without having to look it up; but she can't remember enough to work out whether the feminine would be *femuncula*, or *femincula*. Or maybe *feminicula*. According to Nick, people used to believe men's semen contained homunculi, tiny little men fully formed, that developed into grown people. Anyway, what would a femuncula, or a feminicula, look like? That Hokusai print of *The Dream of the Fisherman's Wife* with that busy octopus, wow, what would *her* feminicula look like? All nips, lips and labia, presumably. Like the Sheela-na-gigs Alyson and her mates gawped at, stifling their laughter, when they went on their week's razzle to Dublin as students. Ah! They stayed in grotty hostels and made idiots of themselves getting rat-arsed with the multitudes in Temple Bar and did the Joyce walk and woke up to monumental hangovers the next morning and generally had an absolute fucking ball.

In a way, Alyson is pleased Anderton discovered her with Boxall. It will hurt him, make him feel her own hurt. Maybe. She thought she loved Jamie, but she doesn't. Anyway, he's ditched her. Bastard.

Why would he be any better than the rest of them? She thinks, I could have gone after him. Then she thinks, *What, go to Canada? Fucking Nova Scotia? No fucking way.* Still, she hates Anderton for how he got rid of Jamie. It was good while it lasted, she felt excited, aroused by the thought of him. It'd been such a long time since that happened.

She gazes at herself in the mirror and the more she looks, the more she seems strange, alien and unknowable even to herself. She wonders if the reflection is more real than the being on this side of the mirror.

This evening she needs to stay up late to finish the preparation for a case. Nick has long since gone to bed. They don't talk much anyway. Not since Boxall. She doesn't want to talk to him. Maybe she will again, one day. She can't keep her eyes open, despite the rounds of black coffee and glasses of wine. She falls asleep in the armchair, her case file beside her on the little table. She dreams she's in a mirrored room and everywhere she looks, it isn't her own reflection she sees but Anderton's expanding form. His wrinkled arse. The flabby roll around his hips, that wasn't there even a few months ago. His belly bulge, still firm. But over time, if he carries on like this, it will probably collapse under its own weight, drooping down in front of his genitals like melted candle wax. She can't escape him.

Once upon a time, she and he would have sat up late talking about all these things to do with the brain, mind, thought, consciousness. Or perhaps she did the talking, and he sat drinking and stroking her thigh and throwing in the odd comment. And they'd drink more wine and talk themselves into bed and fuck each other all night and stare into each other's eyes with a look that said not 'I'm in love with you' but 'I want you, I want you again'. She could lie in bed in the morning on those days, idly fingering herself and coming at the thought of him. Not any more, not for many years, that's why she was so easy for Boxall – ripe for the plucking.

Now Boxall has gone and she hates what Nick has become and what he's doing to himself and what he's done to her. She hates what *she*'s doing to herself. Where will it end? She can't untangle it.

Haematomato

Anderton floundered along behind the trolley and the swaying drip lines and the trauma team in scrubs as they rushed towards theatre. His legs were heavy, his throat felt tight, his chest crushed. He stopped, panted and, after a moment, waddled after them, the fleshy parts of his belly and breasts rolling and shaking with their own unbalancing counter-rhythms. The patient on the trolley was a middle-aged woman whose car had crashed into a tree on a tight bend, and she needed emergency brain surgery. He had to stop again, lean against the wall, and gulp air like a landed grouper.

As he fought to catch his breath, he had a vivid recall of a similar gasping chase along hospital corridors. It would have been eight or nine years earlier, 2007, perhaps, or 2008, a year or so after the Boxall-in-the-bed incident. In those days he was merely overweight and unfit, not yet morbidly obese. He hurries along the corridor, breathless and faint from anxiety. Watches the trolley recede under the glare of the corridor lights, sees the manic squeezing of the oxygen bag. Pursues them with a frantic desperation, afraid of arriving too late. At the theatre doors, they're waiting.

On the trolley, his son Ben.

*

That afternoon, Anderton had been operating on an elderly patient with a blocked shunt when the call came. His secretary had paged the circulating nurse. He was just reaching the point in the operation where he could leave it to the trainee. The nurse murmured in his ear, 'Urgent message from your daughter, says it can't wait.'

'For Christ's sake!' He moved away from the table to make room for the trainee. 'Alex, you can finish off here.' He went out to phone Sophie.

'What's up now? I'm in theatre.'

'It's Ben. He had an accident. I thought I...'

'What kind of accident? What happened?'

'He fell over and banged his head.'

'What on?'

'In the park. Skateboarding. Jumping a bench or something.'

'What did he hit his head on?' There was a note of strained impatience in Anderton's voice now.

'A low concrete wall, I think. His friends brought him home, he was pretty wobbly.'

'Are you with him?'

'I'm downstairs. He went up to his bedroom. He said he had a headache and it was getting worse.'

'Has he been sick?'

'Yeah, all over the bathroom floor.'

'Can you just go to him, Sophie.'

He waited as she went upstairs to Ben's bedroom.

'Listen. Is he conscious?'

'I don't know, I think he's asleep.'

'I want you to do some things.'

'OK, what things?' Her voice sounded tremulous, uncertain.

'Say his name.'

He could hear her call him: 'Ben, Ben. Ben! Anybody home?'

Sophie spoke into the phone. 'He's opened his eyes, but he's not really focusing.'

'OK. Tell him to follow your finger with his eyes. Without moving his head.' After a pause, he said, 'Is he doing it?'

'I don't know. No, not really. I'm not sure.'

'Can he talk? Is he talking?'

'No. Well, kind of mumbling. Not making sense.'

'Get him to move his feet up and down, first one, then the other.'

After a moment, she said, 'One foot's not moving at all, the other one a little bit.'

'Which one moves?'

'Not sure. Left, I think. Yes, left.'

'OK. Listen, I want you to stay with him and dial 999 immediately. When they ask you, say – write this down, OK—'

'Hang on, I need a pen… OK.'

'Say he fell and hit his head on concrete and he's got a severe headache, he's been sick, and he's now semi-conscious. OK? And tell them he's got trouble speaking, and can't move properly. As soon as they get there, get them to phone me. Make sure you say "Professor Anderton, neurosurgical consultant". Can you do all that?'

'I'm not sure. Dad, what if they...?'

'Sophie, come on, darling, you can do it.'

'OK, OK, I'll do it, I'm on it.'

*

Anderton sat on a chair in the corridor outside theatre. Rachel Eaves, his registrar, was scrubbing up to do the operation. He tried not to think about Ben. Another patient was wheeled past on a trolley. Why did the Americans call it a 'gurney'? Maybe someone called Gurney invented it. All those American medical dramas, it was catching on in Britain too. Gurney. The word made him sick with apprehension.

Alisdair Nash appeared.

'OK, I'll take over,' he announced.

'I'm on it,' called Eaves from the scrub room, 'Prof Anderton knows I'm—'

'I will do it,' Nash insisted.

Anderton looked at him.

'Come on, Nick, you know it's best for your son. I'll do it.'

Anderton nodded. He felt as if his emotions had been tied off and cauterised. He wanted to do the operation himself, he trusted his hands. But he also knew it would be a terrible mistake. In the face of problems and complications, and there'd very likely be some, you could not remain cool, professional. You'd panic. That was why you don't operate on family. Nash would be able to maintain the necessary *aequanimitas*. Save Ben's life, maybe. And it was brave of Nash, to be fair. He had little to gain. If things went badly, he'd get the blame. And if they went well, Anderton's gratitude would be grudging, and he'd resent Nash even more, because he'd be in his debt.

What if he dies? What if he dies? Oh, Ben. Not yet sixteen years old. Why, why? Christ.

Anderton hoped Alyson would not come to the hospital. She'd see terrors where there were none: Why's his head so swollen, oh my God, look at his skull, it's grotesque. What are all those tubes? On the other hand, she'd fail to realise the true danger Ben was in. If he survived, and that was in the balance, there was a fair chance he'd have brain damage, and that could change his life, and theirs.

He went to wait in the neurosurgeons' lounge. An hour went by, maybe two. His fear was like a low hum. He felt cold and jittery. His heartburn marauded up his oesophagus. He imagined horrors. Paralysis. Loss of speech. Loss of understanding.

A locked-in state. Years of demented, gurgling half-life for his beautiful boy, his body twisted into weird knotted shapes; another kind of half-life for his family. Anderton had thought the disasters of his *annus catastrophicus* were over. And here he was again, on the lip of tragedy.

The door of the lounge swung open. He had the feeling of someone thrown into an icy sea. He struggled to catch a breath. Nash strode in, still wearing his surgical cap and scrubs. He sat down beside Anderton.

'All fairly straightforward,' said Nash. 'The good news is we took out the clot and found the bleed quite quickly. So we can be hopeful he'll—'

'ICP?'

'Low and falling.'

Anderton started to shake. Thank God. Rising intracranial pressure was one of the great dangers in these situations: the neurosurgeon's dread, and now, here, the father's too. He held his hands tight on his lap, hoping Nash had not noticed the tremor.

'Thank you, Alisdair.'

Nash stood up. 'Don't thank me, old man, it's what we do.' He held out a confident hand. 'Let's see what state he's in when he wakes up.'

Anderton hauled himself out of the chair and shook Nash's hand.

'We'll keep a close eye on him, of course. Always scope for surprises with this sort of thing. As we both know.' He touched Anderton on the shoulder, in control, detached, *aequanimitas* personified, and was gone.

*

Twenty-four hours later, Ben lay in intensive care with lines and wires coming out of his swollen head, his arm. A tube from his groin. A morphine pump, a saline drip. A catheter. Antibiotics. Medication to keep the pressure down. A welt of stitched flesh curving across his scalp, like the seam on a cricket ball. He seemed in a kind of limbo, not quite a person, even to Anderton who was used to all this. He and Alyson stood side by side, staring at their son.

Alyson wept at the sight of Ben's morphed head. 'What's going on?'

'We have to wait,' said Anderton. 'We won't know for some time what exactly is going on.'

He had a memory of a weekend trip to Paris with Alyson, before they had kids. They'd stayed in a dingy hotel near the Marais, went for lunch in a large noisy old restaurant, the kind that was in all the tourist guides. He ordered *cervelle d'agneau*. It was served unadorned and undisguised, a brain on a plate. Alyson nearly fainted. He started to dissect the unappetising grey lump with a dessert spoon, to tease her. 'This is the frontal lobe,' he said, 'responsible for planning, emotional control and problem-solving. It's not highly developed in sheep.' 'Shut up, Nick, I'm going to puke.' 'And this is the occipital lobe that processes nerve signals from the eyes.' He took a spoonful and ate. '*Mmm*. Not bad. Preferable to the sheep's eyes I had in Morocco which were gelatinous, with an unpleasant crunchy—' 'Stop! Just fuck off and let me eat my steak without chucking up.'

He smiled at the memory.

Ben had been stirring on the bed. Now he groaned and opened his eyes for a moment, without focus, and drifted back to sleep again. 'What's causing the damage?' asked Alyson. 'They've got the clot out, he should be improving, shouldn't he?'

Anderton started to explain about contrecoup injury, where a blow to one side of the head sometimes bends the skull inwards, and the impact cannons the soft brain across the cranium to collide with the opposite wall, causing a haematoma to develop over that hemisphere...

'What's a haema-whatsit?'

'Haematoma. A blood clot, from a bleed in the brain. It raises the pressure, which is very dangerous, and starts pushing the brain around inside the...'

She wasn't listening. She was staring at Ben's swollen space-alien head. 'I wonder what's really going on in there?' Her face was crumbling.

He started to reach out to her, to touch and comfort her. She stiffened, seemed to stop herself shrinking away from him; the Boxall wound was still fresh between them. But, with her hands clasped in front of her and elbows pressed in against her flanks, she allowed him to give her a brief hug.

'I don't know,' she said, 'I meant, what's going on in his mind.'

Who knows, thought Anderton. It was hard enough to know what was going on in your *own* mind. How strange it was that an extraordinary amount of activity was happening in the brain all the time, even when you weren't doing or thinking anything. What did they mean, all those regimented networks of neurons, sparking up and talking to each other without your knowing, the incessant chatter of the mind even when you weren't there to oversee it and claim it? What did they mean for who you were? For who Ben was? It was like an orchestra bringing the conductor into being with every performance. For all the advances in neuroscience, all the technological wizardry, nobody had much of an idea of how to answer the simple question: who's running this show? Who is the 'I', if the show carries on regardless?

Alyson grabbed Anderton's hand: Ben was peering back at them, trying to smile through the face mask and the tubes.

'Ben! Darling!' She clasped and unclasped her hands at her breast and moved to his side, unsure whether or not to touch him. 'How are you feeling?'

He lifted the mask away and said, 'What... happened?' His lips were cracked and swollen.

'*Shhh*, darling,' Alyson said. 'Don't try to speak.' She smiled and cried.

'You had an accident,' said Anderton, 'fell off your skateboard, hit your head.'

'Have I had... an... operation?'

'Yes. They took out a big blood clot.'

'Oh.'

'You better put the mask back on. You're going to feel very tired for a long time.'

They left him to sleep and the next day, when they came back, he was already awake and alert. He said, 'Is my skateboard OK?' The consonants came out blurred, as if he were the dummy of an inexpert ventriloquist.

'Oh for God's sake!' said Alyson. 'Haven't you caused enough trouble, you and your effing skateboard?'

Ben grinned.

After a few days, he was well enough to move to the general ward, and then they brought him home. Over the following months, as he made a steady recovery, Alyson took time away from the office to nurse him. Instead of relief at his progress, though, she grew more anxious. Her devotion to his care seemed to be all that was holding her together. At weekends, Anderton tried to take over the tasks of washing and feeding Ben, helping him go to the toilet, working on his therapy routines. But Alyson wouldn't relinquish her duties, and sometimes shooed him away from the bedside. He wondered if it was his punishment for the banishing of Boxall.

Early on, when Ben struggled to string words together, Alyson was alarmed, angry even, as if he were deliberately trying her patience, and Anderton also fretted. He'd insist on conducting tests.

'Why, what's wrong? What are you thinking?' Alyson asked.

'No, nothing, just checking.'

He'd order Ben to touch his left finger to his right earlobe; repeat words such as 'macaroon', 'button' or 'equipment'. Sometimes he'd hold up objects for Ben to name and would ask him to list as many mammals as he could in thirty seconds. Ben would usually comply with amiable patience. If he was halting in his responses, Anderton would take one of Alyson's novels or books of poetry from the shelves at random, read out a sentence, and ask Ben to repeat it. 'Beneath the water of the inrushing tide, the giant clam lay open, ready to feed.' Or 'Returning to the encampment, I told the governor of my discovery.' Alyson also did the readings, sometimes with Anderton in the room. Her choice of book was more deliberate than his. Once, she opened a fat paperback volume at the first page and read, 'Stately, plump Buck Mulligan came from the stairhead, bearing a bowl of lather on which a mirror and a razor lay crossed.' Ben started to say, 'Hey, Ma, that's a bit of a tongue-twister,' but tripped on the very word 'tongue-twister'. He did the thing people do to reset their palate, wiggling his tongue and making a sort of warbling sound. He repeated the word 'tongue-twister', correctly this time, and laughed, delighted with himself, before tackling the sentence again. Anderton and Alyson exchanged a brief smile.

Ben could get frustrated, though, when the words would not come, and grow angry without warning. His mother found it hard to cope with his sudden rages, though Anderton told her it was normal after a brain injury. Ben would swear violently at these moments, but after a minute or two his equability returned, and he seemed unaware of the outburst.

Gradually the speech difficulties receded. After six months, Ben was more or less back to normal, except for a slight slurring of certain words. He said it was like when your mouth was numb after an injection. Anderton thought this was something that would never vanish entirely, like a mild staining, a reminder of catastrophe narrowly averted.

It was some time before Anderton realised that the more attention Ben got, the more difficult Sophie was becoming. When he mentioned this to Alyson, she said, 'Look, it's Ben who needs all my focus at the moment. Sophie will have her time, she'll just have to wait.'

But Sophie couldn't wait. She was slipping into nightclubs under age, drinking spirits in the garden shed with her mates, going for sleepovers at imaginary friends', failing to appear at meal times. She was the mistress of the art of constant, inventive rudeness. Anderton was used to respect, deference even, from those around him, and to having his word become others' actions. Sophie, fully inhabiting her role of difficult teenager, was unintimidated by her father and immune to the norms of deference. Yet, oddly, while he and Alyson rarely failed to wind each other up – with small skirmishes escalating into full-scale battles – he found he was able to respond to Sophie's volatility with calm, side-stepping manoeuvres, avoiding confrontation.

Once, when Alyson was busy going through arduous language routines with Ben as part of his speech therapy, Anderton went up to Sophie's room to tell her to turn down her music. There was no response, so he knocked on the door, loudly. From inside the room, he heard, 'Fuck off will you, we're busy!' He went in. Sophie was lying on the rumpled bed in her underwear, smoking a joint. Next to her on the bed, half covered by a sheet, lay another girl, with cropped hair and a nose stud, smirking at him.

'What's going on?'

They giggled. The girl stuck a bare arm out from under the sheet and took the joint from Sophie. She dragged long and hard, staring insolently at Anderton, before handing it back, turning on her belly, and putting her arms over her head. They giggled some more. To save face, Anderton told them to get dressed, and ordered Sophie to be down for dinner in fifteen minutes. They looked at him, amused and disdainful. He withdrew. A little later he heard the front door close. To his surprise, Sophie did come down to join him.

'Friend of yours?' he asked.

'Dad! Don't be such a…' Her phone bleeped. 'Oh shit, not again,' she muttered to herself.

Before she could return to the attack, Anderton said, 'Sophie, I know it's all a bit fraught at the moment, what with everything going on.'

She put her phone back on the table.

Without anticipating he was going to say it, he added quickly, 'You know what, I was thinking I might book us a little weekend away.'

'OK.'

'In a B&B. Lyme Regis or somewhere. Own rooms, just the two of us.'

'Cool,' she said, and started swiping at her phone again.

The trip was a success. He and Alyson had taken the kids to Lyme for several long weekends as young children. On the drive down, Sophie was like an old-timer reminiscing. Once there, she impersonated a happy eight-year-old child, throwing herself into fossil hunting at Charmouth, feeding the seagulls with stale fish and chips on the shingle beach at Marine Parade, and prodding her father with good-natured teasing. When they got back to London, she soon relapsed into her adolescent provocations. But some of the malice and anger had gone.

*

One night, Anderton dreamed of a figure who was Ben, though not in a fixed way.

Ben was standing on a low wall around the ornamental flower beds on an esplanade, looking out to sea. At the same time, they were somehow at home in London. It was a sunny day. The wind was whipping the waves into a frenzy, with the tide high and rising. In the distance, Anderton could see the skeleton of an old pier. It had a segment missing from the left side. Figures were being caught by the breaking waves and knocked to the ground, then coming back for more, laughing. Or they weren't laughing. They'd been to the dentist and their faces were swollen.

A huge breaker tore up the shingle and over the sea wall, into the ornamental garden. It crashed against the low ledge on which Ben was standing, knocking off copings and collapsing the brickwork. He'd been balancing on one leg when the onrush struck him. The wave carried him out to sea. He seemed to be trying to surf it. Anderton ran down to the shore and saw the figure who was Ben, and not quite Ben, lying on the shingle, vomited out by the waters onto the steeply sloping strand. The boy was covered in bladderwrack and dead man's fingers, like a bedecking of neurons with their axons and branching dendrites.

He could hear the rhythmic sucking sound of the pebbles being tumbled by each retreating wave. He picked Ben up in his arms (he was so light now without all those heavy neurons) and carried him away before the sea could claim him. He laid him down on the esplanade. There was no one about. The sun had gone in, and he began to compress his boy's chest, very fast, one hand on top of the other, pressing down until the ribs creaked like a ship's rigging, one-two-three-four-one-two-three-four... His arms ached, he was sweating, and tears streamed from his eyes.

A man appeared and said, 'Let me do that, you'll give yourself a heart attack.' 'No,' said Anderton, 'my weight will help.' 'I will do it,' insisted the man, 'you'll crush his rib cage,' and he kneeled down, elbowed Anderton out of the way, began compressions. He kept working until Ben coughed and opened his eyes. The water, which was also cerebrospinal fluid, streamed from his mouth and he coughed again. The man had disappeared.

Ben tried to speak but could not. 'Welcome back,' said Anderton. Ben was now lying on a bed, in a sunlit room. He chuckled, and the effort made him splutter until he was red in the face.

'What's so funny, eh?' asked his father.

Ben said, faint but distinct, 'Haematomato.'

'What?'

'It's not a haematoma, it's a haematomato.'

And he laughed again.

He was still laughing when Anderton woke up, also laughing, puzzled but exhilarated. He would tell Ben about the haematomatoes, sometime when Alyson wasn't around.

Alyson

Alyson has the terrors about Nick's possible operation. What if he doesn't make it? How will she cope? What if he does make it? How will she cope? He'll be different. An ex-fat man. Maybe a thin man. As she understands it, the brain isn't self-contained but sends nerves all over the body, including the stomach, the gut. It's all one brain system. That's what she gathers. She could be wrong. But assuming she's right, if you cut out half the stomach, what does it do to the brain, for fuck's sake? Will he be a different person, a different mind, not just a different body?

And whatever the answer to these questions, what use is she to him, the state she's in? She can't even nap in the armchair without wetting herself. And she's had hallucinations. She's asleep, she sees jellyfish, she opens her eyes, they're still there. What next, the DTs? OK, she's been stressed. OK, work has been tough. Nick's been a bastard. She's scared stiff about what will happen after the op, if he has it. But none of those things are the real reason. *The real reason you pissed yourself, and the rest, Alyson, is you drank two and a half bottles of white wine and half a litre of vodka, and you manage two bottles of wine most days, and you can't do without it.*

She's tracked her weight. But she hasn't tracked her drinking.

She knows she has to get a grip. *My name is Alyson and I'm not as high-functioning an alcoholic as I like to think I am.* She's becoming her mother. Except she doesn't even make an effort to hide the bottles.

Earlier today, Sophie rang. After a couple of minutes' chat, she said, 'Have you been drinking, Mum?'

'I had a glass or two at lunchtime. Why, what business is it of yours?'

'I can sort of hear it in your voice.'

'Can you now.'

'I think you drink too much.'

Her own daughter. For fuck's sake. Has Anderton primed her? (Does he care enough either way?) She can't speak for a moment, she's shocked. Then she says, 'Wow. Thank you, Sophie. Wow. *Wow*!'

'Listen, Mum—'

'No, I've heard enough.'

'Look, I didn't mean to upset you, but you need to—'

'Why did you never say anything before, Sophie? For fuck's sake.'

A long silence.

'Sophie?'

A bitter half-chuckle. 'Well, I guess I didn't really like you enough to bother.'

Alyson thinks, Is it about Boxall? Does she know about him? She tells herself it can't be that. It's that her own daughter just doesn't like her. She sobs down the phone. She wails, 'Why?'

'I'm sorry, Mum, but you did ask…'

'Please tell me.'

'You pushed me into saying it. I don't mean I don't like you… I didn't intend it to come out like that, it's just not easy being your daughter, I suppose.'

'I'm that difficult?'

'I don't know, the drinking. All that energy…'

It's Alyson's turn to be silent.

'Mum?'

'Well, thanks so much for that, darling. You've really made my day.' She ends the call and realises she truly does mean 'thank you' – at some level it's gratitude, not just sarcasm.

She needs to talk to Nick. She can't talk to Nick. She phones Ben. 'Are you in the lab?'

'No, you're all right, I'm on my lunch break.'

'Do you think I drink too much?'

'OK. Erm… where's this coming from, Mum?'

'Ben, please. Do I drink too much?'

'I don't know. How much is too much?'

'Ben, just answer the fucking question for once! Pretend you've just had a head injury, say what you really think.'

144

'OK, Mum, if you're going to be aggressive about it...'

'Please, Ben.'

'You want the truth?'

'I do.'

'OK... I think you'd be better off drinking less.'

She hears Ben puff out a long breath, as if it has cost him. She says, 'Thanks.'

'Or avoiding booze altogether.'

'Yes. I think you're probably right.'

Another little step towards a decision. She can't go on. She will go on.

It's exhausting.

She needs a drink.

Bariatric

In the weeks that had passed since the interview
with the clinical director, Anderton had taken a
break, come back no less fat and encumbered than
before, and carried on with his schedule. Nash had
approached him once in the surgeons' lounge, made
a brief cryptic comment about the clinical director's
contingency plans. Was that a hint that they intend-
ed to freeze him out? Anderton felt he was being
watched, even by his friend Bhattacharya, into
whose casual observations he read cryptic allusions
to weight and bariatric surgery.

At least he had the day-to-day business of
operating to keep him occupied and hold the
circling thoughts at bay. This morning's operation
was a complex arteriovenous malformation, a
tangle of vessels in the brain, looking under mag-
nification like a nest of snakes. The patient was a
thirty-year-old woman with severe headaches and
seizures that were disrupting her life, and if she
did not have the operation there was a chance of a
catastrophic haemorrhage.

Once his junior had opened the skull and cut the dura, Anderton proceeded as usual by following the draining vein to the nidus, the snarled centre of the thing. He identified and coagulated the superficial feeder arteries of the malformation, taking great care to preserve the globs of functioning brain around the blood vessels. Now it would become more complicated as he pursued the deeper-lying arteries into the white matter.

Under the operating microscope, the yellow-gold of the coagulating forceps stood out vivid against the red of the vessels and the clumps of white and grey: almost, he thought, like an abstract painting. He squeezed his eyes shut for a moment and opened them again. The field of vision seemed gelatinous and unstable.

'More irrigation, for Christ's sake!' he said to his junior.

The colours and forms seemed to vibrate in front of Anderton's eyes. There was a veil of distance, an indistinctness. He remembered holding out his hand to the scrub nurse for a Penfield dissector to ease away tissue in a convoluted space where he could not see clearly. And then he saw nothing more. He heard the nurse say, 'A number 5?' and he thought, 'Obviously a number 5, damn it!', but he did not hear his own voice speak the thought aloud.

A clang of metal on the floor.

The registrar, high-pitched, nervous: 'Prof Anderton?'

Battacharya: 'Nick, Nick! Are you all right?'

Anderton glared at them. 'Yes, of course I'm bloody all right. I'm fine.'

'No, you're not fine, you just fell asleep!'

'I certainly did not! I'm awake. Is this your idea of a…?'

'You dropped the dissector, Nick.'

A nurse bent to retrieve the instrument and placed it with the other used items. Anderton felt groggy, disembodied.

'Look…' he began.

'Nick, you can't carry on in that state.'

Bhattacharya and the registrar were helping him lever himself out of the surgical chair. His dead weight flopped back again. He was dazed, unsure what was happening. They wheeled the chair away from the operating microscope with him still in it. He heard voices, bleeps going. He might have slept again.

A voice was saying, 'Don't worry about the chair. I'll stand, for God's sake!' It was Nash, furious, summoned to finish the difficult part of the operation. Luckily, he'd been between cases. Anderton heard Nash say, 'How long was he…?'

'Not long, a few seconds, maybe, before we noticed. I think the clang woke him.'

'Has this happened before?'

'No. Not in theatre. But that is once too often, clearly.'

It had also happened outside theatre, in the surgeons' lounge two weeks earlier, waiting to start the afternoon list. Anderton recalled Bhattacharya's hand on his shoulder. 'Bad night, Nick? Come on, it's time to get going.' 'What?' 'Surprised your own snoring didn't wake you up!' 'Sod off, I was practising mindfulness.' 'Of course. In the Hindu mystic tradition and all that.' 'Of course.'

Bhattacharya, his friend, now his betrayer.

Later, Nash came to see him in his consulting room. 'It was an accident waiting to happen, Nick. Bad for you, but happily not a tragedy for the patient. She's fine, you'll be pleased to hear.'

'Thank God. So what now?'

'Let's see what the clinical director has to say.'

'Have you spoken to him?'

'Yes, I have. Pranab has also had a word. We're as one on this.'

'For fuck's sake!'

'What, you expected us to cover for you? When the consultant anaesthetist and your junior and the theatre nurses saw it happen? That's not how this works, Nick, it's not the good old days.'

'So I see.'

'You fell asleep, damn it! You could have killed her.'

Anderton wanted to deny it, to say he'd been resting his eyes, and anyone could drop an instrument. But he knew he would be deceiving himself. He shook his head. 'Why didn't anyone have the guts to come to me earlier?'

'Don't pass the buck! You had a conversation with the clinical director only last month.'

Anderton shrugged. 'Now he's going to send it up to the medical director. Who'll have to contact the GMC, and I'll have my licence suspended.'

'Unless...'

'Unless what?'

'They've offered you the stomach bypass, haven't they?'

'I've said no.'

'Your call. You could always change your mind.'

Anderton expelled a puff of air. He felt ambushed, trapped. He wanted to flail again, hit out at Nash, but he knew he was spent.

'In which case,' continued Nash, 'there's a way forward. You have the weekend to think about it. We're meeting in the clinical director's office first thing Monday morning.'

*

Anderton entered his study and lowered himself into the swivel chair at his desk. He'd woken with a feeling of dread. For a moment it was nebulous. Then the previous day's events came back to him. At the time he'd been too numbed, and later too intent on self-justification, to take in the enormity of it all. But today his failing overwhelmed him. Nash was right: Anderton could have killed or gravely injured the patient. Had he fallen asleep moments earlier, when he had the cautery forceps in his hand, he might easily have destroyed a vein or a nerve, or pierced some eloquent structure. He felt sick at the thought of tragedy so narrowly averted. And ashamed to admit what he had been denying for so long: that his obesity was a danger to his patients.

Now, finally, he had to concede that carrying on as before was not an option. If they took away his licence to practise, his life would cease to have meaning. He would always get up on the morning of a big operation with a sense of anticipation that was almost erotic, and once in theatre, he would be absorbed in the drama and excitement, the smells, the atmosphere, the thrill of deploying rare, finely honed skills. Operating made him feel intensely alive, intensely himself; it was the essence of Anderton. He could not imagine what he'd do without it. He supposed he'd continue to exist somehow, would potter along. It would be a sort of half-life, a twilight zone; without surgery, what would he have left to embrace, except his fatness? He recalled, sourly, an online advert for a resort designed for the obese, somewhere in the Bahamas. It had reinforced beds and loungers, a pool designed to minimise splash, constantly replenished buffets. Photos of happy people parading their fatness, identifying with other fat people with whom they had nothing else in common. As if fat defined them. No, it was not for him.

There were other ways out. Locked in his desk were ampoules of fentanyl and atracurium. Curium as in curare: blow darts, poison frogs... The two together would lead to easeful death. He'd filched them from the anaesthetic room a year or so ago, slipped them into the pocket of his theatre greens. He considered it an insurance policy, forward planning; he'd seen too many patients die in distress. A chemical death was clean and neat – you'd seem to have fallen asleep, relaxed, there'd be no wound, no shock of a mangled body. But suicide was a last resort to end unbearable suffering. He'd dealt with many suicides, attempted and successful, and he'd seen the anguish of the relatives, a world of grief. It wasn't his way. Not now, not yet.

So there was only the one option left. One he resisted, because Nash and the others were corralling him into it, and he disliked that. One he feared, because it meant major surgery, a radical rerouting of his innards, the attendant risks and humiliations. One he worried would make him something other than himself; less weighty in all senses, less imposing, leaving a lighter imprint on the world: a thin man.

Anderton was startled from his thoughts by the sound of a key turning in the lock and the front door opening. It couldn't be Alyson, she was in Manchester. He heard the door shut. He tensed.

A voice called, 'Daddy, you at home? It's me.'

Sophie.

'In here, darling,' he said.

He tried to get out of the chair to greet her, but for a moment he couldn't move. His breath came in wheezing gulps from the exertion.

Sophie came into the study. 'Surprise visit!'

'Hello, darling. It sure is a surprise.'

She walked up behind him and put her arms round his neck, kissed his cheek. He reached up to pat her hand.

'Are you OK?' She examined him sternly. 'You sound out of breath.'

'I'm fine. It's just I wasn't expecting you.'

'Nobody expects Sophie Anderton!' she said, in a mock-dramatic voice.

He laughed.

'Hey,' she said, 'let me help you up.'

'Don't you dare. I'm perfectly capable of doing it myself. Why don't you go and put the kettle on? Or open a bottle of something, I'll be along in a minute.'

As she was going, he called out to her. 'Sophie?'

'Yes?' She stopped and came back.

'What do you reckon to me having the operation?'

'The operation? The stomach bypass?'

'Yes.'

'I thought you said you weren't going to do it.'

'Did I? I don't think I did say that. Anyway, how would you feel about it?'

'Yes. I think you should. Definitely, it would be a weight off everybody's mind.' She put a hand to her mouth and laughed. 'Oh my God, I didn't mean it to come out like that. Sorry.'

'No problem.'

She frowned. 'But I thought you had to have a body mass index of more than 40.'

'I do, near enough, 39-point-something.'

'Oh, OK. But, look, it's your decision. I'm not sure why you're asking me.'

'Because I just wanted...' He halted. He wasn't sure either.

'And why now?'

He thought about telling her the truth, but why overcomplicate things?

'Why *not* now?' he said.

'Fair enough, I guess. Yeah, go for it!'

She left the room, and he picked up the phone and called the gastroenterology surgeon, Phil Rabinovich, at home.

*

The clinical psychologist, a Dr Franks, was alarmingly young-looking, and an idiot.

'Why do you want to lose weight?'

'I don't,' said Anderton. 'I'm indifferent to whether or not I lose weight.'

'Let me rephrase that,' said Franks. 'Why do you want the operation?'

'I *don't* want it. I have to have it if I'm to hold on to my licence to operate at this hospital.'

'*Hmm*,' said Franks. 'And why do you think you became so...'

'So fat? Because I ate too much.'

Franks sighed and wrote something on his form. 'Professor Anderton, what impact would you say your obesity has had on your life? Psychologically speaking, what impact? Self-esteem, relationships, emotional life? How others regard you?'

Anderton thought, How others regard me. He means their moral disapproval of my fatness, their sense of superiority, their right to judge. He was silent.

'The impact on your sex life, perhaps?' Franks pursed his lips, narrowed his eyes, and rested his interlaced fingers on his chin.

'I am fine,' Anderton said at last. 'My relationships are fine. My sex life is just dandy. Fantastic. Explosive. How's yours?'

Franks' eyes flickered. He frowned to himself. 'Professor Anderton, I realise this is difficult for you.'

'Do you?' Anderton pushed down on the arms of the chair and rose slowly to his feet. 'In that case, just sign the bloody form.'

Franks did eventually sign, and some days later Anderton was sitting in the office of his friend and surgical colleague Phil Rabinovich to discuss the details of the bariatric procedure.

'As you know from our last conversation, Nick, there are two main options. Either we staple the stomach, or we construct a bypass from a reduced stomach to the small intestine, missing out a metre or so of duodenum.'

'Either way, it's basically a plumbing operation, *n'est-ce pas*?'

'Always a dab hand at stroking the egos of your friends.'

'Sorry, my anxieties are showing.'

'I can see that. The stapling is simpler, you walk out of here the next day. The bypass is more radical, but the outcomes are far better. And the possible risks are—'

'Will it get the clinical director off my back?'

'Undoubtedly.'

'And see me out? As a surgeon, I mean. Another fifteen years?'

'Should do, I don't know for sure. What do you say to patients when they ask you questions about their partially excised meningiomas, or whatever?'

'I'm parsimonious with the truth.' Anderton thought for a moment before adding, 'That way, at least they'll have a few anxiety-free years before the thing comes back. And besides, one never really knows.'

'Well, then.'

'Fine. Let's do this.'

*

Anderton awoke in the hospital bed thirsty and with a sick headache. Intravenous lines stuck out of his arms. He watched a trickle of yellow urine move along the transparent tube that peeped from beneath the bedclothes. The tube disappeared over the side of the bed, and just beyond he saw a pair of legs in striped navy suit trousers. He looked up. It was Bhattacharya, his anaesthetist.

'Oh, it's you, Pranab. Just when I thought things couldn't get any worse.'

'Yes, it's me, I'm afraid so. How are you feeling?'

'Like death.'

'Excellent.'

'And what are you doing here? Come to gawp at a surgeon reduced to being a patient?'

'Exactly. Very gratifying.'

'You're a ghoul, Bhattacharya.'

'Thank you.'

Bhattacharya looked at him with concerned eyes. For a moment, Anderton said nothing. He held out his hand, not sure why he did so. 'Thanks for coming.'

Bhattacharya took his hand and squeezed it.

At the gentle pressure Anderton felt tears form. 'Well, I'm still alive, as you can see.' He screwed up his eyes and opened them again. 'I hate these bloody ceiling lights, like the ruddy Gestapo.'

'I'm to tell you your wife is waiting outside,' said the anaesthetist.

'Alyson? Christ! I'm not sure I'm prepared for that.'

'In that case I'll show her in. Only wanted to check you were still breathing. You are my meal ticket, after all.' Bhattacharya turned to go.

Anderton called after him, 'You won't desert me for that bastard Nash while I'm out of action, will you, Pranab? He's always trying to poach you for his team.'

'No, Nick. I may flirt with other neurosurgeons, but I'm not actually the promiscuous sort.'

Was that an ironic twinkle in Bhattacharya's eye, wondered Anderton. A gentle dig at his friend's colourful love life? He felt a little emotional. It had to be the effect of the anaesthetic, the morphine pump. He drifted into an uneasy dozing sleep. When he woke again, Alyson was standing halfway between the door and the bed, one arm crossed over her chest, trembling. She was sobbing silently, her mouth puckering. It made her look ugly, he thought. Poor Alyson.

'Hello you,' said Anderton.

She did not move.

'Come closer,' he said. 'I'm not contagious, you won't catch fatness from me.'

She wailed, 'For fuck's sake, Nick, the state of you!'

'Alyson, Alyson. Please, I'm fine, I'm OK. Come and say hello.'

She shook her head wordlessly and wiped her nose on the back of her forearm.

'There are tissues on the bedside cabinet.' He looked at her. 'I'm OK, honestly. I'm going to be joining your thin club.'

At that, Alyson rushed from the room, muttering, 'For God's sake!'

After four days, they sent him home with a pack of multivitamins and an information sheet: 'What to expect after bariatric surgery'. The bariatric nurse came to visit, advised him to take up some kind of activity, preferably social, something suitably gentle on the joints, like yoga or t'ai chi. He growled at her in his severe surgeon's manner: 'I'm not a joiner.' She left him to it. His daughter Sophie took a week off work to look after him, and arranged to share the burdens of care with Alyson at weekends until he could fend for himself.

For a while, Anderton sank into depression, medicalised and helpless. Even though it would be some months before he was noticeably thinner, he felt shrunken and diminished. He had the prospect of a life measured out in puritan portions of flavourless food and vitamin supplements. Over time, as he lost weight, unsightly folds of skin would appear and hang down like baggy clothing. He'd have to get them seen to.

His sense of smell had faded since the operation, and this seemed like the loss of an essential part of him, a neurological deficit, or an amputation even. As a fat man, he'd experienced the world through his olfactory nerve, alert to the subtle perfumes of herbs and spices, the nuances of aged and young beef, of farmed and wild fish, of woodland fungi, Gianluca's truffled pasta sauces.

When he was training to be a surgeon, he learned the aromas of the operating theatre, built them into his repertoire of diagnostic tools. The healthy brain had a clean, fresh smell with pleasant salty top notes of arterial blood and cerebrospinal fluid. The aromatic characteristics of infected flesh were not like those from infarcted flesh, and the precise smell of the former depended on the infectious agent; an abscess laced with *Pseudomonas aeruginosa* reminded him of roast turkey with gooseberry jelly.

His surgical colleagues would dab oil of eucalyptus or menthol on their surgical masks to veil the stink. But he'd wait, poised with his scalpel or his suction device, and sniff the air before extracting the next portion of dead tissue, the next well of pus. He believed his sense of smell made him a better surgeon, and worried that he would now have lost that edge.

He thought of his relationship with Alyson in terms of olfactory decay, from the early optimistic days with their scent of new-cut grass, before the later pooling and stagnating with the repulsive whiff of milk on the turn. He wondered whether there could be a reversal of the cycle such as, on a good day, you experienced in the hospital, where a sick organ had been restored to working order and smelled healthy and fresh again.

*

Sophie came in with a tray of food.

Anderton said, 'You've had your hair cut, haven't you, darling?'

'Yes! Well done for noticing.'

'Well, it is quite... short.'

'Not that short.'

'But nice. Stylish. Suits you.'

'Thanks.'

On the tray was a Lilliputian portion of steamed chicken cut into pieces the size of haricot beans, a miniscule heap of boiled rice, and a few small pieces of carrot. Anderton looked at it without the normal sensory arousal at the anticipated textures of food on the tongue, of the vapours hitting the nostrils. Since the operation, his gut had rebelled against fat. If he ate too much of it, or too much of anything, he'd soon feel the waves of nausea and an unpleasant pain – sick and nervy, yet sharp, as if his stomach would burst – and then he'd have to vomit.

So now he contemplated this plain offering with dismay. 'Where's Ben?' he asked.

'Ben's at work. Pushing back the frontiers.' There was irony in her tone.

'And shouldn't you be at work?'

'Yes.'

'So why aren't you?'

'For fuck's sake. Don't be a pain, Daddy darling.' She smiled at him. 'Now eat.'

Anderton speared a piece of chicken and chewed it without enthusiasm. Would this be his life from now on? He pushed the tray from him and tried to sit up further in the bed. Sophie made to help him but he waved her away.

'He hasn't been to see me since the operation.'

'It's only been a couple of weeks.'

'Four weeks.'

'And he did come to see you, in hospital. We were both there.'

'And you argued. You always argue.'

'No we don't. And if it's been four weeks, you should be up and about more.'

The kids did argue, had argued since childhood. They'd been born fifteen months apart, and had been locked in a fractious stalemate practically since the day of Ben's birth. Sophie's indignation at the dilution of her birthright had turned her from a bright, happy toddler into a whining, demanding one who infuriated her mother. She begrudged Ben his existence. When she was three and he barely walking, she tried to smother him on the sofa; or so Alyson claimed, though she probably exaggerated. Ben responded to his sister with a robust good humour that enraged her even more. 'You're a rabid little pig,' she'd scream. He'd laugh and say, 'You're a rabid skunk, and skunks are smellier than pigs.' At that point she would hit him, and he'd smirk at her.

But now, she was here, and Ben wasn't. Anderton took another piece of food. The carrots tasted of cardboard.

'So Ben's been to see me once in four weeks.'

'He's busy, Daddy.'

'Come on, Sophie, it's not like you to defend the indefensible, especially when it comes to your brother.'

Sophie sat in the armchair, rubbing her hands on her thighs. 'Look, Daddy, Ben can't handle this stuff.' She made a gesture taking in the room, the bed, Anderton.

Strange, he thought, Ben was always the stable, secure one, who took things in his stride, with equanimity. 'What do you mean?'

'He's scared.'

'Scared? What's he got to be scared about?'

'You. Illness. Bodies not working. Mortality. That sort of business. It frightens him that you might stop functioning.'

'Come off it, he's a scientist, for Christ's sake!'

'And you're his father, and he knows what it's like to be... He knows things can go wrong.'

'I guess so.'

They often talked about Ben's brain injury in this style, elliptically. Anderton remembered Ben after his accident, crumpled, taken by surprise by a sudden impact with concrete. He had a fleeting image then of the kite surfer in San Sebastián, blown through the conference window, shocked by the unexpected, terminal harshness of life. Ben, thank God, had survived.

'And he's gently going to pieces,' said Sophie, 'in his calm, secure, optimistic kind of way.'

'And you're not.'

She smiled. 'Is that so strange?'

'Well, Sophie darling, you have been rather...'

'What? Spiky? Volatile? Bit flaky?'

He shrugged, not wanting to provoke her sharp tongue.

'It's funny, isn't it,' she said. 'You know how Ben is always droning on about the way scientists ignore evidence that doesn't reinforce their view of the world. How they explain away all the awkward little facts that don't fit the theory. Well, it's a bit like that in families, isn't it?'

'In what way?'

'Families pigeonhole their members, they stick labels on. You and Mum had Ben down as the clever, brainy, optimistic one, and me as the cautious, difficult, nervy one. Probably just because of that one time when I wouldn't pat that donkey on holiday when I was about four.'

'And the fact that you had some kind of breakdown in your first year at university. Not to mention…'

'I didn't have some kind of breakdown, I had a bad couple of weeks and went to see a student counsellor.'

'And phoned me in a panic in the middle of the night, saying you were desperate and didn't know how you were going to get through till morning.' He looked sideways at her, wary of her reaction at being reminded of that long, fraught vigil.

'Once. I phoned the once. And anyway, everyone has a breakdown in the first year of uni. Then they get on with it. As did I, in case you hadn't noticed.'

'That's true. But it wasn't just that.'

'Meaning?'

'Well, the boyfriends...'

'Come on! What about the boyfriends?'

'That awful chap that wanted to keep you as some kind of decorative, submissive little wifey. And you let him.'

'Charles, you mean? No, you've got it wrong, it was never going to last. It was a phase, I was just acting out a part for my amusement. Charles was a dick.'

'*He* didn't seem to think it was just a phase.'

'More fool him.'

Anderton sighed. 'And before that, the tattooed hipster, whatever his name was, with nothing between the ears.'

Sophie's eyes glistened. 'He had his good points.'

Between the legs, no doubt, Anderton thought. It struck him, oddly, how like him Sophie was. 'And now? Anyone on the horizon?'

Sophie looked at her father quizzically. 'Yes, actually.'

'And what's he like?'

'He's a she, and I'm very happy.'

Anderton, to his own surprise, burst out laughing. 'You're gay? My daughter's gay?'

'I didn't say that. Fluid in what takes my fancy, let's say. Ambivalent. Ambi. Ben would say "polyvalent", or something.'

'Well, well.' Anderton shook his head. 'You are a box of surprises.'

'Aren't we all, Daddy.'

'I suppose. What's her name?'

'Sarah.'

'And you're happy?'

'I am happy. For now.'

'Good.' He reached out and patted her arm. 'Good.'

'Have another mouthful.'

He blew out a resigned breath, like a child made to eat its greens. 'There's no pleasure in it.'

'Please.'

He pronged another piece of chicken. It tasted of nothing except fibrous blandness. He chewed dutifully. He sometimes thought longingly of Le Frattaglie. When he was fitter, he'd go down to the restaurant for a small valedictory glass of wine with Gianluca, tell him that his days of consumption were over. He imagined Gianluca looking hurt, saying, 'Ah, but, Nick, I'm sure I could find you something special. A songbird perhaps? A thrush or two, or an *ortolano*, roasted, with a hint of tomato and lemon, a spoonful of buttery polenta. A mere mouthful...' He could envisage Gianluca touching fingers and thumb to his mouth with a kissing sound, then opening them, and exclaiming, '*Squisito*! Fucking delicious.' He smiled at the thought.

Sophie's voice interrupted his musing. 'You know, Daddy. I might have been a neurosurgeon too.'

'Really? You never showed any—'

'You remember when you used to take me ice skating as a kid?'

'I remember.'

'And in the car on the way back, I'd be asking you things like, "Daddy, why do you have a favourite foot for going forwards in a one-legged slalom but it's the other foot for doing a backwards one-legged slalom?" And you'd say, "What on earth is that when it's at home?" and I'd go, "You know, I showed you just now!" And you'd say something like, "It's all to do with the brain, darling, and anyway, why on earth would anyone want to skate backwards on one leg?" And I'd go, "Daddy, be serious. What's the real answer?" And you'd go, "I *am* being serious." Or I'd ask, "Why can human beings ice skate at all, 'cos they never had to ice skate during evolution from apes? It doesn't make sense." And you said, "People do a lot of things that don't make sense, Sophie."'

'Did I?'

'And I often wondered when I was older, what if you'd given me a proper answer, like you would have given to Ben, about it being to do with brain wiring or, I don't know, the effect of cooked food on brain capacity. Or something. Any kind of explanation that showed you took me seriously. If you'd done that, maybe I'd have gone on to be a brain surgeon. Not some low-grade paralegal.'

Anderton listened in silence, his eyes cast down. He felt a bewildering, unaccustomed emotion. He said, 'You know, I'm no intellectual. I'm not an academic expert on neurology or the evolution of the

167

central nervous system, or whatever. I'm a snipper and a stitcher, a glorified gents' tailor, really.'

'And the son of a butcher, you're going to tell me.'

'Yes. I work with my hands, basically.'

'Come on, Daddy. False modesty does not become you.' She smiled, calm and assured again. How had she crept up on his blind side like this to be the one so in control, poor needy Sophie? He took another piece of chicken and chewed with stoic concentration.

When he'd finished the mouthful, he said, 'Why didn't you tell me all this before?'

'I did,' Sophie said. 'In so many ways. But you weren't in listening mode.'

He'd always regarded himself as attentive to his children, accommodating Sophie's rages and her whims, encouraging Ben's cheerful intelligence. But perhaps he wasn't, or hadn't been. If Sophie could think of him like that, what about Ben? What about Alyson, come to that?

Before the operation, he had, not very consciously, assumed that he would soon resolve the Alyson question. Probably by a clean break. But now things with her seemed less straightforward. The relationship was like a tumour without a clear plane of cleavage, with intricate adhesions to vital structures. Dissecting it away could cause damage and pain to him, let alone to Alyson. Yet, he sensed, things could not stay as they were. He would be a thin man – or, at least, a *thinner* man;

how would she feel about that, having known him fat for so long?

He wanted to talk to Sophie about all this. But she'd say something like, *Don't be silly, Daddy, you and Mum will never split up.* Or she'd cry, or something.

As if reading his thoughts, Sophie said, 'And you were never very attentive to Mum, either, to be honest.'

'I tried to be. At least I think I did.'

They sat in a silence which Anderton broke by asking, 'And am I now?'

'Are you now what?'

'In listening mode. Attentive.'

She narrowed her eyes, severe and blue like his. 'Time will tell.'

'You're a hard woman, Sophie.'

They both smiled. But he knew Sophie was right, that he had neglected Alyson. Yet something strange had happened to her since his surgery. It was as if she'd said to herself, Even that lardy man-mountain has taken responsibility for who he is, so I can too. And to the amazement of Anderton and the kids, she'd booked herself into an addiction clinic in Godalming. 'It'll never last, it never does,' Anderton had muttered. Sophie had snapped at him, 'Don't be like that, Daddy. It's as if you want her to fail. And even if she does, at least she's trying.'

Yes, that was true: at least she was trying. If she did dry out, would he be able to cope with a newly confident Alyson? Perhaps she'd look for a younger model. And if they were neither of them as before, would that give them a chance to build something more positive, less self-destructive? Or would the things that bound them together dissolve, leaving nothing at all? He didn't know. *Time would tell*, as Sophie might have said.

Some weeks later, Sophie brought Sarah to the house. Sarah looked almost Italian. Though she was skinny like Sophie, she had intense, voracious eyes that reminded him of Alyson in her twenties, and she stroked her girlfriend's arm with a tender lasciviousness, observing Anderton the while with her raw gaze. To his embarrassment, he felt the first serviceable stirrings of lust since... since when? It seemed like years. A stimulus, a response. *Eppur si muove*. He thought of Alyson, with a twinge of guilt. Could she ever provoke those feelings in him again? It was possible, if she stuck to her new regime. He felt a wash of adrenaline and, like fog burned away by the sun, his post-operative gloom began to dissipate.

*

Nicholas Anderton faces the mirror, dressed in jogging bottoms. For years after he got fat, he saw himself as having the body of a trimmer man. Now he still sees a fat man, though he is hardly that any more, and finds it ludicrous that his limbs and trunk fit into clothes that are surely too tight, too small. Intellectually he can see, though his belly still strains a little at the fabric of his T-shirt, that his features are sharper and his chin less buried in flesh. But it is difficult for him to believe in this new truth.

He is upright, his weight on his right leg, his hands one above the other, palms facing, as if holding an imaginary football. He extends his left leg to the side, cocking his foot, bending the knee and shifting his weight to the left, rotating his upper body while inverting the position of his hands to turn the imaginary ball through 180 degrees. He breathes deeply, and reverses the move, slow, controlled, coordinated. He has a certain grace, heavy but compelling, in sympathy with some unheard beat.

He feels more solid, more *Andertonesque*, than for years. He has *aequanimitas*. Even as he performs the slow, stately movements, a part of his mind is wondering where in the brain *aequanimitas* is located. Does it sit where the emotions are, in the amygdala, or in the mysterious reaches of the limbic system; or where personality is formed and dissolves, in the folds of the frontal cortex? Would it be possible to pinpoint it with stereotaxy and stimulate it with probes?

Tomorrow morning at seven o'clock, he will be in need of *aequanimitas*, a full measure of it. He is to return to theatre for the first time since his operation. He will perform a couple of simple procedures, replacing blocked shunts, helping his registrar to drain a subdural empyema. Gradually, he will build up his confidence again, his precision, his operating muscles, and that arrogant bastard Nash can like it or lump it. In a few months, maybe less, he'll be back near the peak of his powers. And no longer fat. That will take some getting used to.

Acknowledgements

I would like to thank several people for their help:
Alan Mahar for his insightful editorial dissection
of my first draft, and for his rare ability to see both
the big picture and the detail; Miles Larmour for
his customarily brisk line-by-line suggestions; colleagues from the excellent Tindal Street Fiction
Group, where I workshopped early versions of
several of the chapters; my wife Diana Foster
and sons Daniel and Joseph Ferner, who listened
patiently to some or all of the work read aloud and
made useful suggestions.

My medical siblings Robin Ferner and Rosalie
Ferner, and sister-in-law, Celia Moss, enlightened me
about hospital life. I also benefited from the advice of
consultant neurosurgeon Nick Thomas and consultant gastrointestinal surgeon David Gourevich. None
of these experts are responsible for any technical
howlers, for which I claim sole credit.

In researching the world of neurosurgery, I found
the memoirs of surgeons instructive, both about

the medical issues and about the psychological and emotional sides of a surgeon's life. It would take too long to list all the books and the many academic and popular articles I consulted, but the following works were particularly helpful: Fred Christensen, *Stopping the Pain*; Katrina Firlik, *Another Day in the Frontal Lobe;* Atul Gawande, *Complications: A Surgeon's Notes on an Imperfect Science*; James Geissinger, *Memoirs of a Neurosurgeon*; Henry Marsh, *Do No Harm*; Danielle Ofri, *What Doctors Feel*; Frank Vertosick, *When the Air Hits Your Brain*; and Gabriel Weston, *Direct Red: A Surgeon's Story*. I spent many hours watching brain operations on YouTube, and am very grateful to the surgeons who post educational videos of their procedures. I can only wonder at the order they bring to the apparent mess and chaos inside that daunting and mysterious bone box.

FAIRLIGHT MODERNS

Bookclub and writers' circle notes for all the
Fairlight Moderns can be found at
www.fairlightmoderns.com

SOPHIE VAN LLEWYN

Bottled Goods

When Alina's brother-in-law defects to the West, she and her husband become persons of interest to the secret services, causing both of their careers to come grinding to a halt. As the strain takes its toll on their marriage, Alina turns to her aunt for help – the wife of a communist leader, and a secret practitioner of the old folk ways.

Set in 1970s communist Romania, this novella-in-flash draws upon magic realism to weave a tale of everyday troubles that can't be put down.

*'It is a story to savour, to smile at, to
rage against and to weep over.'*
- Zoe Gilbert, author of *FOLK*

*'Sophie van Llewyn has brought light
into an era which cast a long shadow.'*
- Joanna Campbell, author of
Tying Down the Lion